Bolan was pressed hard

At least three more shooters were on the other side of the pickup truck. He'd been in this position before and he wasn't about to panic.

He drew back from the Peugeot, putting ten yards between himself and the vehicle to get a better view of what was going on. Four gunners were making slow advances. They were concentrating on the truck, and not beyond it. He unleathered the Beretta, slipping a fresh magazine into it. He was going to get as many of them off guard as he could, and the pistol, though at the extreme of its range, was the only tool for this bloody trade.

This mission wasn't finished, but the Executioner was back on the road to seeing justice served.

MACK BOLAN ®
The Executioner

The Executioner®
Don Pendleton's

AGENT OF PERIL

A GOLD EAGLE BOOK FROM
WORLDWIDE®

TORONTO • NEW YORK • LONDON
AMSTERDAM • PARIS • SYDNEY • HAMBURG
STOCKHOLM • ATHENS • TOKYO • MILAN
MADRID • WARSAW • BUDAPEST • AUCKLAND

First edition February 2005
ISBN 0-373-64315-2

Special thanks and acknowledgment to
Doug Wojtowicz for his contribution to this work.

AGENT OF PERIL

A glorious death is his
Who for his country falls.

—Homer
Iliad c. 1000 BC

I am the Executioner. I have done what no soldier has ever done. My wrath is turned against those who are the enemy of the innocent. If you want to stop me, you'll have to kill me.

—Mack Bolan

To the soldiers who gave their lives in
Operation Iraqi Freedom. The critics and the cynics
can debate the why, but your how was impeccable.

Prologue

The soldier did a flip over the slab of cracked, pockmarked stone, heartbeats ahead of the slashing rain of incoming fire. Bullets hammered the rock with incessant fury, trying to reach the flesh that had escaped them only moments before. Glancing around, he realized he was in a bad situation, surrounded on all sides by grim, determined enemies. Rubbing his gravel-stung cheek, he saw the shell of an old building, but his enemies, armed with grenades and assault rifles, would blow him out of that ruin easily, if they didn't slice him in two in the first place. This was nothing new to the grizzled veteran, muscles drawn tight as he prepared for yet another brutal clash.

He pulled the clip from his Uzi and saw it had only five shots left. He poked up his head, but his enemy was out of sight. He narrowed his eyes, knowing that they were gathering courage to make their move.

"You might as well give it up! You're surrounded and outgunned!" the invisible enemy called out.

"Bring it!" It was a simple invitation.

That's when he heard the pounding footsteps. Weapons sounded on the other side of the stone, cries ringing as the enemy charged.

He had to time it exactly right.

The weapons stopped popping and the soldier rose, swinging his Uzi. The pause in the shooting, he hoped, was

Agent of Peril

the end of their supply of ammo and they'd have to reload.
Five shots, one for each pull of the trigger, flew out of the
barrel. One, two, three enemies went down, screaming as
their chests were stitched, but one was still left charging,
struggling to recharge his rifle on the run, feet pumping as
he surged forward.

"Hey, you kids!"

The illusion was broken in an instant. The paintball sailed
wide and to the right as the pistol snapped off its pellet.

Liev de Toth was no longer a soldier pitting his might
against the forces of evil; he was just a teenaged boy on the
West Bank, playing with his friends. The jolt of reality was
ice water, cooling him off from gleeful excitement. As he was
on the downward surge of play-induced adrenaline, fear cut
in and spiked him up again.

Old Man Strieber had to have heard the gas-powered
sound of the paintball guns as they spit their pellets. Liev
snapped his head around and picked up his scratched and battered Uzi. It looked like a real soldier's weapon with duct
tape and tattered cloth around the stock. The scratches only
added to its character.

Strieber was getting closer, moving as quick as his bum
knee could carry him, which was still quick. He'd taken a
bad fall and tore the ligaments while a paratrooper in the
army. When he wasn't busy growing apricots in the field,
he still exercised and trained his farmhands and whoever
else would come to learn the art of using a rifle. The old
soldier didn't approve of paintball gunning, said it wasn't
a safe way to train, but Liev and his friends liked the fun of
it. The fact that Liev hadn't been shot in a half dozen ses-
sions, even against huge odds, added to the teenager's feeling that running and gunning with the paintball guns was
of vital usefulness.

"C'mon Liev! Let's go!" Raffi shouted, and Liev raced

away from Strieber's equipment shack and back toward the settlement in the valley.

"We almost got you today, man," Jan spoke up as Liev joined the knot of friends.

Liev took their shared gym bag and threw his gun in with the rest of them. "When I sign up, I'm going to be one hell of a soldier. Look out Hezbollah!"

Liev was going to say more when he felt a deep rumbling in the ground. He paused, looking back at the Strieber farm.

One at a time, the five teenaged boys stopped, looking back at the three churning trails of dust snaking and writhing into the sky. There was something familiar about them that eluded the youths for a moment, but the accompanying sound, akin to some metallic beast incessantly clearing its throat, brought the knowledge to life.

"Tanks?" Liev asked. "Here?"

"Maybe it's maneuvers," Jan said, unconvinced even by his own argument.

"That doesn't make sense," Michael answered. "They're coming from the south. Why are they going that way? They should be taking the main road."

Noah gave his friends a small push. "Look!"

The tanks weren't skirting the orchard; they were plowing through the center of it. Liev's jaw dropped as they spotted the trio of tanks tear through the small grove of apricot trees, smashing their trunks to splinters under their grinding steel treads.

"That's insane! What do those idiots think they're…" he shouted.

Suddenly gunfire began flashing from the turret.

Old Man Strieber had a half dozen farmhands on the porch of his squat ranch house, watching in shock as the orchard was ground to sawdust and pulp. They had no idea what was going on until the first muzzle-flashes erupted.

Coaxial guns swept them with sheets of lead. Three undulating threads of slaughter ripped through the ranch house's aluminum siding and flesh alike, the aluminum bursting and popping open neatly, gutting insulation and shards of wood underneath. The six men were not so neat and tidy as flesh and bone exploded, blood spraying across the front of the building, bullets continuing through, unabated by their time in a human body, to smash and puncture yet more aluminum and wood.

Strieber came running up the other side of the road. It was impossible to believe that only heartbeats earlier, Strieber had driven the boys away from the pile of stones and rotted wood he kept behind his equipment shed, where the boys had been feigning war. Feigning the hellfire that was now hammering real death, blood and thunder to the drumbeat of heavy machine guns.

The top hatch on the right-most tank popped open. Liev tried to make his mouth move, to scream a warning to Strieber. His throat had turned to a cracked riverbed, dry and burning as he tried to get more than a hoarse whistle past his tonsils. The gunner in the commander's cupola spun the machine gun mounted there, swung it down on Strieber and tapped off a long burst.

Liev watched in disbelieving horror the atrocity going on before his eyes. Strieber disintegrated under the storm of .50-caliber rounds.

"Run!" Liev shrieked, finally forcing words past his lips with Herculean effort. His friends took off, legs pumping, like bats out of hell.

The ranch house detonated into oblivion under the impact of the tank's main gun.

The shock wave gave Liev an extra bit of push.

Steel damnation was on its way.

1

Mack Bolan crawled across the slate, low shrubs concealing him as he pulled his improvised sniper's drag bag behind him while keeping an eye on the temporary auction lot a half mile distant.

The Executioner was tracking a trio of traveling Hezbollah, led by Bidifah Sinbal, a veteran organizer and moneyman for the Lebanon-based Palestinian terror organization. They had been moving a lot of cargo on a freight ship from Lebanon to Pakistan. The freight was being unveiled on a slab of granite adorned with ammunition crates and assorted military vehicles. Bolan couldn't see into the massive cargo containers that Sinbal's men were opening, but he saw the look of awe on the faces of the men who swung open the gates on the three massive containers.

Something nasty was in there.

Bolan swept the area with a field scanner, checking for motion. He slipped like a ghost along the very edges of the field, disturbing little as he crawled along the path.

Bolan's battle gear was limited. He'd been able to smuggle most of his nonlethal gear across borders as he raced to get ahead of the freighter. However, the Executioner's signature pistols and his heavier weaponry were left behind. Bolan had left his usual weaponry in a diplomatic pouch, ready to be forwarded anyplace that he needed more firepower for a long-haul mission.

This day the Executioner made do with what he'd bought at a tribal gun shop in Peshawar. He had plenty of money for some hand-built, if eccentric, weapons.

The primary weapon was a hand-tooled Short Magazine Lee Enfield—the classic SMLE of the British forces during World War II. The weapon was topped with a Chinese knock-off of an ECLAN scope that gave Bolan some reach. The pistol-gripped rifle was a smooth shooting machine. For more hectic work, Bolan had also bought a 9 mm Skorpion machine pistol and a pair of stainless-steel Brazilian Taurus PT-92s. The Taurus handguns were almost identical to his Beretta 93-R, lacking only barrel length, a folding foregrip and a 3-round burst option. The Peshawar gunsmiths even managed to retool the Taurus to operate with the Beretta's extended 20-shot magazines. Still, they were somewhat different from what he usually carried.

That didn't matter.

It wasn't the tools that had allowed Bolan to survive against insurmountable odds for as long as he had. But they sure helped.

Bolan swept the fighting field and wondered what his course of action should be. He wasn't sure what he'd find, following the trio. They'd come ashore at Gwadar, more than nine hundred kilometers south, but thankfully in the age of satellite telephones and satellite surveillance, the Executioner was able to keep tabs on the massive boxcars as they were loaded onto train tracks from Gwadar to Nok Kundi to Quetta, where they were offloaded.

Bolan was racing to intercept them from the north, having managed to snag a transport flight into Afghanistan and stopping off with American U.S. Army Special Forces. The Special Forces operational teams were dividing their time between restoring the nation in their role as teachers and diplomats, and on the side, still hunting for leftover madmen from the Taliban. The Executioner wished those men luck, and left them to their task, knowing that it was in good hands.

The Hezbollah trio was a danger that he had taken unto himself. They had picked up a good-sized bodyguard force during their train trip. Now the three moneymen were accompanied by a dozen well-armed men. Bolan didn't know them by their faces, but if he transmitted their images back to Stony Man Farm, he was certain that he'd come up with local al Qaeda loyalists.

Bolan wanted to take another close look at the Hezbollah bunch.

They were talking, moving out of the way as the contents of the first container came rolling out.

It wasn't the chill of the Pakistani spring winds that Bolan felt in his bones as he saw the familiar boxy frame of a tank rolling out of the boxcar. He wanted to believe it was a Soviet tank, or some Chinese knockoff, but his eyes and mind were already placing the unique frame and shape of the armored vehicle. His stomach curled into a knot. He didn't want to believe what he saw, but there it was.

An M1A1 Abrams tank. The main cannon was disassembled, and from the range Bolan was looking, it was an older model, with the old 105 mm gun instead of the newer 120 mm gun that was the mainstay of the United States armed forces. This was cold comfort, as the tank was still an almost unstoppable war machine, capable of laying waste to an entire city before an air strike or other tanks could be brought to stop it.

Three boxcars.

Three tanks.

The terrorists could easily barter themselves up to seventy-five million dollars for the sale of these war machines to anyone who wanted a small armored force. And it wouldn't take much effort to convert the old 105 mm cannon into the more modern 120 mm pieces that could cut through an entire building with one shot. Bolan set down the SMLE and checked his arsenal. He didn't have a single thing that could make the odds anywhere close to equal against even an empty Abrams with half a tank of fuel. The forty pounds of C-4 explosive might be able to dent one tank, but to destroy all three…

The waiting game was over and Bolan swiftly began setting up his first shot with the SMLE.

Destroying tanks with a .30-caliber rifle wasn't something he planned for, but he did have eighteen stripper clips of .303 ammunition for the SMLE and he was mentally setting up the long shots to cause mayhem and destruction. Armor-piercing rounds were filling the magazines.

Bolan brought the scope to bear on a stacked crate of 67 mm artillery rockets. He reckoned the distance as around 400 meters, and brought the rifle's point of aim up enough to compensate, then pulled the trigger. The SMLE shoved against the Executioner's shoulder. Thick cedar burst apart like flimsy plywood as the 124-grain tungsten-cored slug slammed into the contents of the wooden crate. What happened next shook the ground, but the Executioner was already looking for new targets, throwing the bolt back to feed a fresh .303 into the breach.

With both eyes open, he saw the bowl of smoke rising, a blast zone easily forty yards across. Screams of panic rang out as the terrorists ran for cover. Spotting a fresh target, Bolan pumped a second round through the fuel tank of a motorcycle. Fuel sprayed wildly from the burst bladder, and the gunman atop the bike slipped, tumbling to the ground. Bolan dropped his aim and sent off a second round almost immediately after the first, skipping the third .303 round off the fuel-soaked tarmac. The bullet hit with a flaring spark, and gasoline flashed in a fireball, washing over the guard.

Panicked bodyguards whipped out weaponry from wherever they had it stored and more than a few began blasting at each other. Bolan swept along, burning off the rest of his first magazine, taking shots that nicked or sparked close to already hyper alert gunners.

A few bullets here and there got the maddened gunfight going. Bolan threw back the bolt one last time, then stuffed down ten fresh rounds and closed the rifle, swinging for more new targets. One of the weapons auctioneers was screaming, pointing frantically toward him. The Executioner might have ignored him except for the RPG-7 rocket launcher being aimed in his direction.

With a single stroke of the trigger a bullet slammed into the rocketeer's groin, tearing through his pelvis with sledgehammer force. In the same instant, the severely injured gunner squeezed the trigger on his weapon, bending halfway over. He skipped the 77 mm warhead off the ground, firing too soon to slam it point first into the earth. The teardrop-shaped warhead deflected and went skidding along the tarmac, giving the detonator time to arm.

In an instant, the point of the rocket struck the treads of the Abrams tank. On impact, the shell went off. The explosion wasn't the earthshaker that the Executioner started the show with, but Bolan saw one of the Hezbollah moneymen go skidding away, his feet turned to greasy streaks in their wake. He cried out, pistol in hand, clawing toward a suitcase full of money and firing aimlessly in rage.

The Hezbollah group had been chopped in two. Bolan had seen the fifteen-man force brought down to nine by the warhead's explosion. If he was going to get any answers on the tanks, he needed to start taking the moneymen alive.

One was firing off the contents of his weapon into the wounded RPG gunner, stitching him with 9 mm pistol rounds. Bolan tagged him in the shoulder, blowing the back out of the joint with a .303 round and knocking him down. He swiveled and punched a second round into the face of a gunman who noticed the moneyman go down. Gunfire sizzled back and forth as the Executioner turned his weapon and aimed at the crates that the RPG gunner drew his shells from. The .303 round sailed and hit wood, but nothing happened. Bolan cycled the action and shifted his aim slightly.

This time RPG shells shattered the earth and sky in a chain reaction, one hammering explosion after another, sending shrapnel, flame and splinters flying in an ever growing cloud of devastation. Bolan rose, slinging his war bag. He ran hard toward the caldron of chaos and confusion and cut the distance between himself, and the destruction by half.

After reloading Bolan dropped to one knee. He snapped the rifle to his shoulder and burned off ten shots as fast as he could. The first rounds went into the tires of a jeep whose driver was trying to get himself, some customers and their goods, either bought or to be sold, the hell out of Dodge. The vehicle swerved hard and flipped.

The unlucky driver's passengers went flying from their seats, and crushed crates vomited out rifles that were ground and shattered between the overturned jeep and unyielding asphalt. A desperate buyer froze in the headlights as the vehicle went skidding out of control at him, and found himself pinned as it slammed into him and crushed him under the tail boom of a Dauphin helicopter.

As Bolan was reloading, he spotted the drumlike extension on the wing stub of the Dauphin, reminiscent of the artillery rocket launchers of the old Vietnam helicopter gunships. On a hunch, the Executioner swung and aimed at the drum and pumped four .303 rounds into the launcher. The fourth shot gave the Executioner results as the helicopter disappeared in a massive shock wave.

The sales ground was sprayed with even more shrapnel

and fire. Panicked buyers and sellers raced about, security men and bodyguards firing brutal bursts into one another.

A little panic goes a long way, the Executioner thought, scrambling closer to the battleground after feeding the Enfield some fresh rounds. A spray of bullets smashed into a rock off to the soldier's right and he went to the ground, feeling pebbles stab into his ribs and knees, elbows barking on stone.

Bolan shouldered the Enfield and spotted a half dozen men working their way toward him. A second spray of autofire was a massive sheet sweeping through the air, pounding and deflecting like copper-jacketed rain on the barren hillside. In a heartbeat, the front sight of the Enfield was on the lead gunner, a .303 round punching through his chest and bursting out his spine in a single gore blast at a range of seventy-five feet.

Bolan threw the bolt and turned on another gunman. Slugs from the security man's Uzi sliced the air, kicking up chips of slate and granite as they bounced off the ground short of Bolan's position. The soldier took care of that situation with a single decapitating .303 Enfield round that hit the killer's throat. Bolan rose and was moving hard to the left, bullets chasing him.

The Enfield dropped on its sling around the Executioner's neck as he swept up the Skorpion from where it hung and held down the trigger. The 9 mm rounds spit at the enemy hardforce, four men scrambling for their own cover as they sent lead his way.

Unfortunately, the Skorpion rattled apart in a savage, recoil-induced field stripping that left the Executioner's right hand numb with shock. He should have known the knockoff would prove useless. None of his rounds hit anything, though they did drive the enemy to cover.

Curling his right hand to his belly for protection, Bolan

snaked his left hand around, freed one Taurus and straight-armed the 9 mm pistol at one of the Pakistanis who was rising again. A chopped-off AK-47 in the gunman's hands swung toward Bolan's midsection as he saw the tall, powerful terrorist charging him.

The Executioner's sole saving grace was to get within bad-breath distance of the enemy fighter. He tripped the trigger on the Taurus twice, bullets slamming hard into the hollow of the terrorist's throat and his chin. Jaw shorn away, the guy whirled, his AK tumbling from lifeless fingers. By the time the others were adjusting their aim against Bolan, he went to the ground again right in the middle of the three remaining men. Bullets swept the air from one overanxious machine gunner, autofire ripping like a steel storm through his two comrades as he tried to track his executioner.

Bolan rewarded the wild man's efforts with two bullets through his groin and one in his stomach.

It was about then that Bolan started getting feeling back in his right hand. It hurt like hell, but he could move the fingers, and looking around, he saw three severely wounded gunmen, their fight gone, blood pumping out on charcoal-colored rock. Testing his weight on the right hand, Bolan got back on his feet and spared a single 9 mm bullet into each dying man's head, granting them a swift release from their pain. Bolan was not a man to leave an enemy to suffer, no matter what they did.

A quick reload, and the Taurus went to Bolan's right hand. He crouched and grabbed the chopped-off AK of the man he charged, as well as a pouch of magazines. Satisfied the weapon was in working order, he holstered his pistol and found the rifle was an AKSU in 5.45 mm Soviet. With the stubby barrel of the chop job, the rounds would put out a fireball the size of a watermelon, but wouldn't have much more punch than a Magnum pistol, and have very limited range.

But the gun wasn't going to shake to pieces and bruise Bolan's battered hand any worse.

The Executioner looked over and saw that the Hezbollah hardforce had picked up a bunch of new shooters, and they'd noticed the conflict on the hillside. The range couldn't have been more than sixty yards, and even for the most ill-educated thug, the math couldn't have been difficult.

There was a stranger approaching in the wake of the destruction.

He was armed.

Bolan hit the ground again, using a large piece of debris for a shield as bullets raked the side of the hill. Sparks flew as copper jackets hit granite and flint, and crimson puffed skyward as slugs impacted on stilled corpses. The Executioner fisted the AKSU and poked it over the piece of metal, firing the contents of the clip already in place. It was a full load, and three seconds of mayhem swept in response to the crackling salvos downhill.

A bullet hammered into the frame of the AKSU and sent it flying again from the Executioner's hand before he could pull it back to reload. Not wasting a moment, Bolan tucked tight and rolled, rocks stabbing along his body as he scrambled behind a flat plate of stone. Another wave of hellfire hammered a nearby corpse, reducing the lifeless body to a pulpy stew. Surrounded and outgunned, Bolan didn't have many options. He took a look at the slab of granite he was behind and felt its thickness with his fingertips. Thick enough to stop enemy bullets for a while.

Long enough, Bolan realized, for his enemy to flank and kill him.

The hollow that he rested against was curved. The soldier could work with that. He wouldn't have much of a chance, but it was a thread of hope. He began packing C-4 into the hollowed cavity, flattening the kilogram blocks like putty in three strips, kneading them like dough. Bolan pulled a radio detonator and plugged a wire into each strip, sticking it to the center patch of explosive.

Bolan poked up his head and saw the enemy was charging. He pulled both Taurus pistols and dived backward away from the rock, scrambling in frantic retreat. The pistols barked out hot 9 mm pills until the left one ran dry. A couple slugs plucked at the Executioner, and one bullet hammered into the Enfield's stock, cracking it against the soldier's ribs. A bullet creased Bolan's elbow skin, not touching bone. He probably had as much accuracy as his enemy.

On the run, the enemy had no aim as they charged, a small favor to the Executioner as long as they were at a decent distance. If they got closer, though, he was hamburger.

The nearest gunman was almost at the rock that Bolan had mined.

The soldier dropped his left Taurus and slapped the radio detonator's switch. The hill shook before him, and the shock wave nearly blew out his eardrums.

While Bolan was slammed by a pressure wave, his enemies fared far worse. The granite slab that the plastic explosives were jammed into fragmented instantly, shattering like a fine crystal goblet under the force of a sledgehammer. The shards of the slab didn't just sit around, however. Thrown at 1500 feet per second, in a widespread cone of bloody murder, the pulverized stone became a gigantic shotgun round.

Whether the chips of granite were blunt pebbles or razor sharp, they still went through human flesh like hot knives through butter. The lead gunner, jumping onto the rock, sailed through the air over Bolan's head, slamming into the hillside headfirst.

Where once there were men, suddenly there were ghosts, the debris wave flashing at them, then passing on, bloody stumps standing in the wake of the improvised Claymore. The whole scene was a panoramic widescreen display in Bolan's pressure-wave-shocked brain. His perceptions warped in time and space so that he could see the pulped cores that used to be humans pouring and melting down to the ground, any pretense at being a solid long stripped by the brutal death wave that crushed through them.

Bolan felt the back of his head, scalp split, blood flowing hotly down the neck of his black BDU blouse. He sensed a concussion, but he sat up, reloading his last remaining pistol. The other Taurus had been lost, swept away in the shock wave. He looked for signs of the enemy.

Everything was still, except for one squirming figure, trying to crawl up the side of the Abrams tank. Staggering to wobbly feet, Bolan got up, feeling weak and dizzy. He had business to attend to before he could tend to his own scratches and scrapes.

Bolan pressed some gauze against the back of his head, looking around at the spread of bodies. Anyone left standing had run like hell. They had to have been convinced that missiles were raining down on this little bazaar of death. Sure, the terrorists were escaping to fight another day, but for now they were frightened.

And being frightened was three-quarters dead. Good enough for a bleeding, limping Executioner.

Bolan recognized the guy climbing the tank. It was the Hezbollah moneyman who'd lost his feet. There was something familiar about the guy who scrambled like a drunken spider. Getting to the tank, Bolan casually reached up under the man's suit coat and grabbed his belt.

"Come here," he growled, yanking the terrorist off the tank. The footless killer squealed as the back of his head bounced on the flattened and cracked concrete.

"Bastard..."

"That's what they call me," Bolan said. He knelt on the hardguy's chest, lifted the stainless-steel Taurus and let swing with a savage stroke. Already, his brain had cleared enough to recognize Bidifah Sinbal.

"A long death or a short death," Bolan said. "Your choice."

"Generous offer. I give you nothing."

Bolan looked down at Sinbal, then realized that droplets of blood were pouring onto the guy's face with every exhalation of his own breath. The soldier put the back of his hand to his nose and came away with a glove of sticky, slick fresh blood.

"Looks like you overdid the explosives, punk." The terrorist chuckled, lying on his back, wheezing as he finished off his laugh.

Bolan sighed. He was too dizzy and hurt to conduct a proper interrogation on Sinbal. The Hezbollah savage wasn't going anywhere.

The Executioner got to his feet and climbed up the side of the tank, calling back to the wounded terrorist.

"Sit. Stay."

Inside, the mystery of the first generation M1's origins were revealed.

Outside, flags and insignias were scoured off and replaced with desert paint that broke up the graded and scaled camouflage pattern of the metallic beast. Inside, however, the writing on the controls was in Arabic.

The Executioner knew only one modern Arab military force that used the U.S.-built armored vehicle.

Egypt.

Hezbollah was in Pakistan, selling three Egyptian tanks. Bolan crawled up through the hatch once more, wiping his nose. The bleeding had stopped. He was still hurt, hammered and beaten.

But someone was moving top of the line tanks around like they were common contraband.

That was a someone the Executioner had a vested interest in shutting down—permanently.

It was time to call the Farm.

2

The flat LCD screen popped up a still image of the Executioner's hawkish features, giving Barbara Price something to visually focus on as the satellite phone connected them vocally.

"Did I catch you after a full night's sleep, or are you delusional from Bear's coffee?" Bolan asked.

"Mix and match." Price sighed. "What's wrong?"

"Lots. I've got three M1 Abrams tanks. I'm thinking they're U.S. military aid package tanks because they have the old 105 mm cannon instead of the new 120 mm tubes," Bolan told her.

"Abrams tanks?"

"The Hezbollah operatives I followed had them transported here for the auction."

Price summoned recent intel-footage on her second monitor. "We had three M1s roll into a Gaza Strip settlement and kill a few hundred people."

"A tank attack on the Gaza strip? Where?"

"Nitzana."

Bolan paused a moment. "If I remember my map of the space between Israel and Egypt well enough, it makes sense to strike there. Nitzana is far from any other major settlements. Vast expanses of empty hills, desert, and desert farmland surrounded the settlement."

"It took twenty minutes for the Israelis to scramble aircraft."

"A few hundred people?" Bolan asked.

"The count is 249 dead, another three hundred missing, and over twelve hundred injured. They blew up buildings… Hell, they even blew an F-16 out of the sky. That crash killed almost fifty people by itself," Price said.

"Three hundred missing, which means that we could see the death toll get over four hundred as a conservative estimate," Bolan said.

"Most of those missing are from a school and a hospital that the tanks shelled," Price told him.

"Children and the infirm."

Price knew the tone in Bolan's voice—grim and torn. He was getting ready to revisit hell on the kind of savages who would drag the innocent and helpless into their petty political games.

"Striker, how many tanks did you say you had?"

"Three here. With Arabic writing on the controls. I'm looking for a good way to dispose of them, but I don't have the kind of firepower needed to take them out."

Price turned. "Hunt, I need a way to dispose of three M1 tanks without bringing the entirety of the Pakistani military down on whoever's blowing it. They might think it's India."

"A Force Recon off the USS *Stennis* is stationed in Tora Bora. They can chopper in hot and fast, set daisy cutters on each vehicle and be out before anyone knows what's going on," Hunt Wethers stated. He managed a grin. "I've got Captain Hofflower on speed dial."

"Send them on in," the Executioner said.

Price heard a wet sniff on the other end of the phone. "What's wrong? You sound…sick."

"Got too close to an improvised Claymore mine I made. Or rather, didn't get far enough away from it," Bolan answered. "The shock wave broke blood vessels in my nose and I'm bleeding all over."

"Why can't you get nasal drip like most people?" Price asked.

"Just get the team here quick. I've got a live prisoner, and he's Hezbollah."

"Striker, you're going to hand over a member of Hezbollah to a Marine?" Price asked.

"This animal's buddies killed a few hundred people. Including children. I don't care what the Marines decide to do with him."

With that, the phone went dead.

PUSHING HIS TONGUE between his upper and lower molars, General Nahd Idel forced his lower jaw to relax, but the clenching muscles were relentless. His personal physician had tried all manner of muscle relaxants and therapy, but that didn't help. A mixture of stress and old rooted pain from a botched wisdom tooth removal had given him a case of lockjaw that he couldn't kick.

Idel jammed several sticks of gum into one cheek and looked at the aide who was finishing his report about the "terrorist raid" on Nitzana.

"They're saying that at least a quarter of the dead were Egyptian or Palestinian," Major Pedal Tofo concluded. "Hezbollah won't be so darling with some of their friends because of this."

"No concern," Idel replied. "Why did they only attack with three tanks? Didn't we give them a dozen?"

Tofo shook his head. "We have people who are in Lebanon. They were watching Sinbal and his men leave Beirut on a cargo freighter with six oversize boxcars. He only left three in Alexandria, and stayed with the freighter. Records list the ship en route to Gwadar, Pakistan."

Idel bit his tongue, muscles swelling and straining. Outwardly, his face remained impassive, but inside, he was strung as tight as a bear trap. He sat up and squared off a stack of paperwork on his desk, making sure the corners were sharp on the pile. Come to think of it, the jaw clenching could have just been another symptom of the obsessive-compulsive disorder that drove him to be the perfect officer, and kicked him through the ranks of the Egyptian military.

"Sinbal took three of our fucking tanks out of the country?" Idel asked.

"We gave him the tanks. Any money he'd get selling them would be pure profit," Tofo answered.

Idel stood and walked to the window. Sunlight burned outside, flaring off the almost white sands surrounding his base's compound. He took a deep breath, then spit out his gum, lighting a cigar to chew on. Grinding his teeth into the fat tobacco roll made him feel better, the sponginess cushioning his aching jaw muscles.

"Do we have anyone who can do a wet operation on Sinbal when he returns to Lebanon?" Idel asked.

"Affirmative," Tofo stated.

"Make sure Sinbal doesn't spend an evening more in Beirut without a bullet in a major part of his anatomy."

"A pleasure."

"That said, how did the three tanks do?" Idel asked.

"Reports have 375 dead so far, 250 missing, and thirteen hundred injured," Tofo reported. "The border between Egypt and Israel has been locked down, and the Gaza Strip and West Bank are under heavy military patrols at this time. Combat aircraft are on constant patrol, too."

"Their armored divisions?"

"They've brought up two divisions, in the north and the south to cut off access to their coastal settlements."

"Only two?"

"Others are in motion, and a third is passing by Nitzana and has set up temporary camp across the Nitzala River."

Idel smirked. "They're wondering if Cairo had anything to do with an attack on their stolen territories."

"Or they're simply not taking chances. Israel might be outgunned by her enemies, but she makes up for it by not fucking around."

"Good. Good."

"Have we been given any green light by Cairo, sir?" Tofo asked.

Idel looked over his shoulder, pulling the cigar from between his lips and stretching out his jaw. He let his ears pop before continuing. "Would it make you feel better if we had our benighted leaders' support?"

"I'm already dedicated to the cause of getting back Egypt's lands from the Israeli thieves. I merely worry that…"

"We will be seen as traitors and thieves if we are caught. I understand, Pedal," Idel said, clapping his aide on the shoulder. "We won't be tied to the events that turn the cold peace between Egypt and Israel into a hot war. But we will be there at the forefront when it is time to be heroes and take back what is rightfully ours."

Tofo nodded. "I do not doubt you, or this plan."

Idel smiled and took a drag on his cigar.

But if Tofo truly didn't doubt the success of the plan, he was the only one in that room.

THE STRAPPED FOR COMBAT SH-60 Seahawks tore over the landscape, penetrating deep into Pakistani airspace. Captain Carlton Hofflower perched in the doorway of the lead chopper, eyes sweeping the horizon for an angry response coming over the horizon. Nothing, however, was turning its attention toward the quintet of helicopters this day.

The message from HQ was quick, simple and terse.

"Retrieve Colonel Stone. Bring lots of explosives. Coordinates to follow."

"Captain. We have smoke," Lieutenant Charles Ellis, the pilot, reported.

Hofflower's hazel eyes focused like lasers on the spiraling rub of charcoal smearing upward into the blue over the rolling hills. He didn't need a map to equate the billowing smoke to the location of Colonel Stone. "That's our guy, GPS be damned."

Ellis glanced back at Hofflower, and then returned his attention to guiding the Seahawk.

In moments, the sharklike chopper was splitting the sky over the smoldering battlefield, and Hofflower could see a conflagration. Two major blast craters, and a half dozen minor smoking pits plumed smoke skyward, while one man stood with an old-fashioned bolt-action rifle over an injured man.

"That's Stone?" Ellis asked.

Hofflower nodded.

"Who's the wounded?"

"I don't know, but he doesn't look like a friendly. Tell the other choppers to land in a diamond around this airfield," Hofflower said.

Hofflower gave Ellis's helmet a tap, and the SH-60 dropped to the ground, landing with a light bump. As always, the six-foot-six Marine captain "unassed" first, hands resting on the M-249 hanging from his neck and massive shoulders.

"I have a present for you," Bolan stated in lieu of a greeting.

"I see. Middle Eastern, Lebanese by chance?" Hofflower asked.

"Yeah," Bolan returned.

"Bidifah Sinbal. Works for Hezbollah," Hofflower said. The Marine grinned and cracked his knuckles. "Colonel Stone, this is a wonderful gift."

"I want to know where Sinbal got his tanks from, and if it was his people that were behind Nitzana," Bolan said.

An interesting question, the Marine thought.

He intended to make Sinbal squeal and spill his guts.

IT TOOK TWENTY MINUTES for a medic to clean and dress all of Bolan's injuries, but during that time, the Marine Force Recon platoon was busy wiring up the M1 Abrams tanks with enough explosive power to chop them to splinters.

Inside, even more insidious devices were being planted. The insides of the tanks would be able to survive the destruction of the hull and engine section. Nothing short of a nuclear weapon would pulverize every component of the tank in one shot, and even then, the M1s were designed during the Cold War. Their very design was meant to get the massive steel beasts through a nuclear-explosion blasted war plain and continue fighting, even as atomic artillery shells created football field-sized craters all around them.

The Marines were putting miniature Fuel Air Explosive charges inside the tanks. The mini-FAEs were designed for house clearing the easy way. First, a burst would spread a cloud of fuel through a space as large as a single floor of an apartment building. With the air saturated with explosive fuel, a second burst would spark and ignite the atmosphere. Everything within the space would be vaporized.

Bolan had seen entire mountainsides crumbled with a Fuel Air Explosive device improvised from a simple propane tank.

The mini-FAE would smash every ounce of valuable electronics and design inside the M1 to useless pulp. The last thing the world needed was a reverse-engineered version of the U.S. Army's best tank.

The Marines were meticulous in setting the charges on the armor, though. That was the one thing that Bolan was most concerned about. Abrams armor, indeed any modern tank armor, was a secret design, and each nation had its own proprietary formula. Having that secret drop into the lap of even an ally was considered a disastrous development.

"I'm done," the medic said. "You can stop the Zen meditation."

Bolan managed a weak smile. "I was just thinking about the tanks."

"How the hell did these get here?" the medic asked. "I mean, Pakistan uses old Soviet T-72s."

"They were brought by the Hezbollah, and the Hezbollah somehow got them from Egypt," Bolan answered. "How they got them, I intend to find out as soon as I get some intel."

A gunshot rang out and Bolan turned his head. The sudden reflex action filled his head with sloshing, hot liquid pain, but it was dying down and his equilibrium swiftly returned to normal. It took a moment for his brain to register the sound as a .45-caliber pistol. Captain Hofflower was returning, stuffing his MEU (SOC) custom 1911 into its holster with one hand, holding a small black box with the other hand.

"I recorded everything," he said, tossing over the digital recorder. Bolan caught it with one smooth motion.

"Make sure that someone sends me a new recorder. With all the features," the Marine captain said.

"How much did he have? Nutshell version," Bolan said.

"Well, he helped load the van with explosives for the 1983 Marine barracks attack."

"That was more than two decades ago."

"He's forty-three. And he's been Hezbollah since he was a teenager," the captain explained.

"The tanks?"

"Given to him by his commander. He doesn't know exactly where they came from."

"Who's his commander?"

"A creep named Faswad."

Bolan closed his eyes and reviewed his mental files. Imal Faswad moved into the Bekaa Valley after Bolan rampaged through to take out a terrorist-backed drug cartel. He'd been behind some major counterfeiting of American hundred-dollar bills, approximately fifty million worth, before the U.S. Mint updated to the new bills. The Hezbollah headman was someone who was never quite on the top of the Executioner's "to do" list because he was mostly attacking people who could, and did, fight back. Bolan's previous interest in Faswad was derailed when the guy's headquarters was blasted to atoms by an Israeli air strike and a dozen thousand-pound bombs.

It looked like it was time for the Executioner to pay Mr. Faswad a visit to find out why he was suddenly selling off tanks.

"Who did Sinbal come to sell the tanks to?" Bolan asked.

"Somewhere in the piles of grease you left littered all over the place, there was a party of Filipinos who are, er, were with Abu Sayyaf."

Bolan's jaw clenched for a moment. Abu Sayyaf was aligned with al Qaeda. Another case of unfinished business that the Executioner would have to get to.

"You sure I got them?" Bolan looked around. "A lot of guys just took off running."

"Well, give me a good DNA lab, we'll know for sure," the Marine replied.

"All right. I'm lucky I got a single prisoner for you to interrogate," Bolan conceded.

"Thanks for helping bring a little justice to the Corps," Hofflower said, putting out one beefy paw.

Bolan took the hand, remembering what felt like a lifetime ago, his own incursion to avenge Marine blood. He could feel the bond with the fighting man before him.

"It's time to unass and blow this Popsicle stand," Hofflower called out, pulling Bolan effortlessly to his feet. "It's good to have you aboard, Colonel."

"Thanks," Bolan answered. They got into the Seahawk and Lieutenant Ellis pulled the chopper into the sky, rising a half mile before stopping.

Hofflower handed over the radio detonator to the Executioner. "Your prerogative, Colonel."

Bolan accepted the detonator, flipped up the safety cover on the firing stud and thumbed it down. Even through the rotor slap and vibrations of the SH-60's powerful turbines, the shock wave from detonating the tanks was palpable. Concentric rings of smoke, indicating the rippling forces that devastated the armor, were still visible down below.

That was just the opening salvo to the scorched earth process being undertaken.

The four orbiting Marine Seahawks were armed with artillery rockets and Hellfire missiles. Pilots and gunners opened fire instantly on the ground where the terrorists sought to sell the Devil's tools. Explosions formed a scouring cloud of devastation that swept from the four corners of the auction ground toward the middle, shredding and splintering anything in its path. Stomped flat as if under the feet of giants, the hodgepodge mixture of surviving jeeps, guns, helicopters and low-speed jets, as well as various missiles and other explosives, disappeared in a cacophony of devastation that Ellis yanked the SH-60 out of just in the nick of time.

Bolan could almost reach out the side door and touch the blossoming mushroom of smoke from the hell blitz.

An explosive start to a mission that promised more such devastation ahead.

3

It was time for the weekly mail drop, and J. R. Rust, posing as a journalist, stepped up to the cage, smiling.

"Your new cameras and printer are here, Mr. Russel," Rudiah, the mail clerk, notified him. He was wrestling a box onto the counter.

Cameras and printer? Rust thought. The box looked fairly large. "I hope the editors thought to include an instruction manual this time," he said.

Rudiah almost said something, and then smiled tightly.

Yeah, the Lebanese post office wasn't at all interested in what James Russel was receiving in the mail from America, Rust thought sarcastically. He looked at the return address and saw it was from Egypt, but labeled from a blind intel dump that a man named Striker had set up with him. Rust had worked with Striker and a covert strike team on two dangerous operations, one in Pakistan, and one in Lebanon, racing to deal with forces ready to blow the Middle East wide open in a nuclear conflict.

Since then, Striker had tapped Rust personally, knowing that the CIA man had his ear firmly planted to the ground in regards to Middle Eastern politics and terrorism. Born eating and breathing the cultures of the Islamic nations from the Mediterranean through the Kashmir, Rust was an expert not only in Arabic dialects but mannerisms and mind-set. This ingratiated him to the movers and shakers of the nations he frequented. Either as an invisible part of the embassy staff, or, slightly more out there, as a journalist, Rust was able to blend in, become a fly on the wall, and get information to the ears that needed to hear it.

Rust thought about the need to get information to the right ears, and thought of 2001. Maybe that was why a veteran CIA man was so willing to buck the system and risk his job by leaking information to a phantom not even the Company was sure about. Striker went to the field and actually put boot to ass.

He signed for the box. The damn thing weighed a ton.

Hauling it under one arm, he left the post office. That's when he saw a dark-featured young man out of the corner of his eye. Rust's alarm bells went off when he knew that the young guy didn't fit in. There was something wrong about him, but he couldn't place what.

Things were really tight now. Unbalanced and hindered by the heavyweight box, he couldn't rapidly reach the tiny Glock 26 he had nestled in an ankle holster. He knew how to draw quickly with the ankle rig he wore, but that was with his hands free and his ability to turn unhindered by a big, heavy box. The CIA man was of a mind to just dump the box, but that wouldn't be good for his health if the package contained a bomb.

"Russel," a voice called. It had a mixed Midwestern and South Florida drawl to it, and Rust had to look twice at the man who spoke using the voice.

It was the guy who set off Rust's instincts. The features were a little too dark for Egypt, and not hooked enough to be fully Semitic, but he did look like he fit in Lebanon, even though his manner was that of a Westerner. The hair, though, was nappy and short to his head, and dark eyes studied him carefully.

"Russel, I'm here on ranch business," the man said. His hands were occupied, filled with a rolled newspaper in his left and a bottle of water in his right.

Rust relaxed. It was kind of an unwritten code among the agents in the area that they have their hands filled when they met, to distinguish friend from foe. Empty hands meant that the person you were meeting wanted his options open to immediately grab a weapon. The plastic water bottle and newspaper, however, were indicative of a savvy mind—they could be dropped with no hassle, and guns could be grabbed as trouble arose.

Ranch business was another clue. It was a code phrase that Striker had used with him in their private dealings.

"Let me set this hunk of crap down and we can talk somewhere," Rust answered.

The handsome man smiled, and easily slipped the bottled water and newspaper into the deep pockets of his cargo pants. Reaching out, he took the box. "I'll carry that."

He could see the younger man's dark arms ripple with corded muscle. "Oh sure. Just because you're young, strong and agile…"

The kid grinned. "Old age and treachery will win over youth and purity every time."

"I like your attitude, kid."

"Just want to live long enough to get to old age and treachery, Mr. Russel."

He nodded and led the way. "Got a name?"

"Alex Johnson, sir."

Rust paused and looked him over. "You look like a Johnson."

"Excellent, sir. I was barely able to detect the sarcasm in your tone."

"Come on, Alex."

ALESSANDRO KALID SET DOWN the cardboard box with a grunt, causing the rickety old table to wobble under the sudden impact. Kalid held his breath for a moment, but the spindly legs held. In the heat, it was heavy work, and he was glad for the breeze that pushed and puffed-up the gauzy drapes to Rust's apartment. He didn't know how much was in it, but knowing the man he knew as Striker, the box certainly wasn't filled with jelly beans and Easter eggs. He looked at the seal on the box and saw the telltale signs that the tape had been stripped off and replaced.

"Someone's been looking in Striker's stuff," he muttered.

"Yeah," Rust stated. "The Lebanese have been interested in the packages that come in to me."

Kalid flipped out his Tanto knife with a deft wrist movement, slashed open the box and returned the blade with a flourish. "If that's the case, your cover might be blown."

"That's on the short list of things that are certain in life," Rust answered.

Kalid could only shrug and pull out the contents of the box. "A laptop, a printer and some digital cameras."

"Son of a…" Rust said.

Kalid smirked. "The printer works, but it's twice the size it should be."

He flipped over the unit and looked at the bottom. "No, not smuggling guns."

"So what's that?" Rust asked, pointing at the silver square that Kalid was removing from the printer's plastic shell.

"Consider it the ultimate in wireless modems. State of the art. I think I'm supposed to light my eyeballs on fire for knowing about this," Kalid said. He looked through the heavy booklet in the box. "And the manual on how to use the cameras."

Kalid flipped through the book. "You think they'd slip something into this that could give us a clue as to what's going on?"

Rust held out his hand, and Kalid handed over the book.

"The manual's copyright page," Rust spoke up after a moment. "There's a user name and password for the laptop."

Rust powered up the laptop after plugging it in to the modem and the wall outlet.

Kalid watched Rust type the access into the computer, then looked out the window.

More than the gauze curtains were moving. Traffic had cleared off the street, as had most of the women and children. Kalid's brain went into overdrive as he saw two blurs flying through the air. On pure reflex, Kalid drew a shaken throwing star and flipped it at one blob, knocking it back, slowing it in midair enough to determine the identity of the object. It was a cylinder, with writing on the side, smoke spewing out the top in a gout. Somewhere in the distorted adrenaline overdrive of the moment, Alex Kalid recognized the tear gas projectile. One part of his brain wondered what the second object was. Reflex, however, threw his mouth wide open, screaming loudly to Rust.

The cry of alarm saved Kalid's brain from a battering from the concussion grenade's explosion. The second blurring minibomb had sailed through the window and landed under Rust's chair. The thunderclap of pressure was brain numbing, shaking Kalid's hyper-perception back to something resembling normal.

Rust was on the floor, his chair collapsed, eyes open and dazed, the laptop spilled across his chest.

"Yeah, your cover's blown," Kalid quipped, lips engaging on their own while his hand reached for his knife. He wondered where his gun was, the concussion knocking away the memory that his SIG-Sauer P-226 was back at his hotel, in a hidden compartment of his luggage. He snapped out his arms to each side, corded muscles bracing him against the disorientation.

His brain stopped sloshing in his head after a few heartbeats, his vision clearing. His gaze locked on the door, which shuddered under an impact. Dust and splinters fell from the door and its frame, and Kalid realized he had only one more smash before whoever was on the other side swarmed in and took them. He glanced around. Rust looked back at him, eyes unfocused from a point-blank concussion, then lifted one leg, trying to bring it up.

Kalid noticed the pistol in the CIA agent's ankle holster. He lunged, grabbing it off the dazed man's leg and swinging it up. No safeties, no bells, no whistles, even punchdrunk, Kalid knew it was a Glock of some kind and he opened fire, not even waiting for the door to crash open. The door splintered again, but the second impact didn't have the force of the first after Kalid slammed four shots through it at chest level. A rent appeared in the top panel, a jagged shard bent out by whatever battering ram was being used. He could see the men in the hall scrambling and tending to their wounded.

Kalid opened fire again, sweeping the hallway for another eight shots before the 12-shot magazine on the Glock ran dry. With the little pistol at slide lock, the door was slammed again. This time, it buckled and burst inward. Two men rushed in and the ex-blacksuit spun the Glock in his hand and hurled it at the first one through the door. Despite being a lightweight gun with a polymer frame, the twenty ounces of steel in the gun still made a big impression on the forehead of the first thug through the door. The intruder went stumbling to the floor while the guy behind him leaped, snarling and bringing up a pistol, as if to stuff the gun in the American's face.

Kalid grabbed his wrist and drove his palm into the guy's elbow, leveraging him and tossing him against the wall with a bone crunching thud. The pistol went flying across the floor, but Kalid wasn't going to give up any advantage over even a dazed enemy while he might still be able to stab him in the back. Instead, he brought up his knee hard, two quick pumps into the kidneys of the captive Lebanese, then dropped back and twisted.

The terrorist went sailing out the window, catching the half-open pane on his way out, as well as the gauzy curtains. Glass, wood and fabric enveloped the falling man as he went tumbling into the street twelve feet below. Kalid pivoted on his heel as he heard the scrape of steel on steel in the doorway.

A big, bearded man had a long curved fighting knife clenched in his fist. His face was drenched with blood, but there were no visible injuries on him. Kalid assumed he had to have been behind another guy who took a high velocity 9 mm pill.

"We were going to try to take both of you in alive, but Faswad only needs one prisoner," the knife goon sputtered.

Kalid smirked and answered him in his own language. "Quit talking and bring it, crybaby. Papa doesn't have all day to play with children."

Crybaby gawked at the taunting response, and paused. That gave Kalid a half step to grab his knife from where he dropped it by Rust. Then the Lebanese knife fighter charged, swinging at chest level. Kalid dropped like lightning, first to scoop up the blade, and second to snap his foot out into the shin of the blade man. The minute his fingers met the handle of the Tanto, he brought the blade around in a fast arc, only to have his wrist trapped by the half-fallen Crybaby.

Bringing his weight to both feet in the crouch, Kalid swung up his left hand and hammered it into Crybaby's face, feeling cartilage crunch and collapse under the impact. It seemed the complaining Lebanese was made of stern stuff, as he kept up his fight, bringing his knee into Kalid's shin to knock his balance from under him. The curved knife arced up, but Kalid braced his forearm against the knife fighter's forearm, the impact jangling nerves in both arms. Still, the fighting knife didn't fall from numbed fingers, and Kalid had to wrap his hand around the bigger man's wrist.

There was no time for a wrestling match, not when the guy could roll onto him and drive that foot-long tusk of curved steel into his chest. With a surge of strength, the ex-black-suit launched his forehead into his enemy's nose. This time, the impact stunned Crybaby, his head rolling back onto his shoulders. Kalid hurt from the hit too, but it was minor in comparison. He slapped the knife away and pulled his own wrist free, punching forward with both fists to slam into the man's rib cage.

The big terrorist rocked backward. Kalid scrambled to his feet and out of reach. No more wrestling against someone who had a weight and leverage advantage. It was time to employ some sharpened steel in the fight.

Kalid lunged and lashed out hard, blade poking from the bottom of his fist. The blow was a little short, the tip of the Tanto only parting skin, not muscle and bone as the slash connected with the upper torso of the guy. Crybaby grunted and brought his blade down, but Kalid had moved enough that the downward swing only nicked his shoulder, instead of plunging into his clavicle. He brought back his knife and turned away, luring the Lebanese terrorist in closer.

As soon as the first boot stomp sounded, Kalid continued with his pivot, bringing up one heel hard and fast, connecting with the knife man's groin. As Crybaby grunted, Kalid finished his total 360, slashing savagely with the Tanto across the exposed neck and shoulder of the enemy knife fighter.

The Lebanese grunted as he clutched his wounded shoulder. The knife dropped from his numbed fingers and Kalid stepped in, carving a fatal slash across his adversary's face and throat.

Kalid stepped back, and watched the dead man hit the floor.

He looked up. The doorway was suddenly crowded with a throng of angry-faced men, their fists filled with automatic weapons. Kalid set his jaw tight, clenched his knife tighter and glared back at them.

"My life will not be sold cheap!" he shouted.

Suddenly, the gunmen in the hall began jerking, going into what seemed to be epileptic fits as puffs of gore burst into the air all around them. Automatic weapons fire chattered in the hallway. One by one, the dead gunmen tumbled to the floor, their perforated corpses stacking atop one another in a bloody heap.

Kalid felt a moment of terror as he realized how close he'd come to death, and looked to see if he could find the lost pistol on the floor when a large form filled the doorway.

Mack Bolan dumped the empty magazine from his Uzi and fed it a fresh one. Kalid saw an array of fresh bruises and cuts on his face, but he still managed to have a smile on his face at seeing a comrade in arms.

"Grab Rust. We're leaving the laptop behind," he told Kalid.

"The chase is on," Kalid said under his breath.

4

Bolan recuperated from his concussion on the flight from Afghanistan to Lebanon. What with a two-hour helicopter ride, and arranging an airplane from Kandahar to Beirut burning another three hours, the Executioner had enough time to feel the throbbing in his head come back down to a manageable level. With more hours of sleep on the plane, and years of athletic endeavor tuning his body's recuperative powers, he felt almost healthy. None of this counted the couple hours where he was X-rayed and given a tetanus booster at a field hospital. He still ached from head to toe, and his multiple stitches tugged and pinched if he moved too quickly.

Bolan supplemented the stitches on the gunshot wounds on his arm and legs with duct tape to pin everything in place. It was a cheap way to make sure the skin wouldn't flex and pop the stitching open, and it reinforced the closing power of the nylon loops. He couldn't do anything about the sew-job at the back of his scalp, however. He was just glad that there was no skull fracture. The original brain swelling from the concussion was also not evident on the X rays.

Good news all around, he thought sardonically.

But now J. R. Rust was among the walking wounded, though he seemed to be getting better.

"Can you hear me, J.R.?" Bolan asked as he and Kalid loaded him into the back seat of a Toyota 4Runner in an awkward balance of speed and gentleness, neither of which was completely accomplished. The Executioner still kept his Uzi by his leg, just in case, looking up and down the alley.

"How'd you know we'd be in trouble?" Kalid asked.

"I took a look at how dead this street got when the two goons at either end of the road cleared it out."

"What goons?" Kalid asked.

"The ones who threw the grenades and caught some 9 mm bullets," Bolan explained.

"Ah. That's what kept you."

"I only cleared this side of the alley. We're going to have to run a gauntlet," Bolan told him.

"I'll drive, you shoot," Kalid said.

Bolan nodded, the desire to chuckle driven away by the dull pain in his head. He admired Alex Kalid's acceptance of life with the Executioner at his elbow. They'd only worked together for one day some months ago, but the young agent proved he had the blood of a soldier running in his veins.

Bolan slipped into the shotgun seat next to Kalid. "Drive."

Kalid gunned the engine and swung the 4Runner onto the street. Almost instantly, a shout went out, and gunfire popped downrange. Rust gave a loud grunt and tucked himself tight into a ball in the back seat as something hammered the side of the 4Runner. Bolan spared a glance to see if Rust was all right, and confirming his party was still unharmed, whipped up the Uzi and tapped out a short burst at the gunner sending fire at the SUV as it whirled.

The gunner wasn't hit. Bolan knew he didn't make the connection on instinct, but the short burst did drive the terrorist to ground, sending him out of their path. Dust kicked up on the dry street as Bolan kept watch for more gunners, but the terrorists were clearing out. The soldier knew that sticking around when the Beirut police were in the area was idiotic for both sides.

In the time since the Executioner's last visit, the country had cobbled together again. The discord and chaos in the streets was under control, a nation unified and ready to tolerate no dissent. Sure, terrorist organizations hid among the country's nooks and crannies, but Lebanon knew that if they didn't control violence in its territory, Israel once more would surge across the border to do some cleaning.

And Bolan knew that cleaning didn't involve feather dusters and furniture wax.

"Keep moving. We'll drive around for a while," Bolan told Kalid.

"No destination, Colonel?" the ex-blacksuit asked, using Bolan's Brandon Stone identity.

"Yeah, but I want to check for tails first," the Executioner explained. "Looks like Hezbollah knew about J.R.'s cover identity."

"And they only acted when there was a big signal marker that someone was coming to see him," Kalid replied.

"Not necessarily," Bolan countered. "You okay, J.R.?"

"I'll live. I'm just now getting my hearing back," Rust answered. "Which code name are we using, Striker?"

"Striker or Colonel Brandon Stone," Bolan answered.

Rust nodded, holding his head. His vision was still unfocused, and Bolan knew that Rust was suffering from a concussion. He sympathized with the CIA man; he'd just been there. But he still needed the sharp mind that had just taken a beating. "I heard that the Hezbollah was jumpy because Sinbal never phoned home from the yard sale he went to."

"And then they see a possible CIA plant getting forty pounds of something at the local mail drop, something super-suspicious," Kalid groaned. "Just perfect."

"Your cover was already smoked, J.R.," Bolan stated, apology flavoring his tone. "I didn't intend for either of you to get hurt."

"Fuck that shit," Kalid answered. "I signed on to this to break some heads."

"Like the chicken said, I knew the job was dangerous when I took it," Rust agreed. "That's why they pay us the big…er…pathetic bucks."

Bolan nodded, accepting their allegiance. A moment of hope surged in his heart with the bravery of these two men, then he settled down to check the mirrors for signs of pursuit.

"OUR MEN TRIED TO PICK up Russel, but they met with resistance," Cabez informed his leader, Imal Faswad.

Faswad shook his head. "Resistance? I sent two dozen men after the American."

The Hezbollah leader took a deep drag on his cigarette, and then blew smoke out of a corner of his mouth. "Two dozen men. How many came back?"

"Six," Cabez answered. "They think they recognized one of the men involved."

"Really?"

"He was over six feet tall, with black hair and cold blue eyes."

Faswad paused for a moment. "Black hair and cold blue eyes?"

"Familiar to you?" Cabez asked. "That's the description of al Askari."

"Not only that," Faswad answered, "it's the description of the man who paved my way to leadership here."

Cabez allowed himself a moment of surprise, but then relaxed. "The Soldier has rampaged several times through Lebanon, sir."

"Perhaps this could be the time he comes for me," Faswad stated. "Sinbal never reported in, did he?"

"No, but we have reports from our friends in Pakistan that

something happened to the weapons auction. The place was utterly destroyed, and scores were mowed down like wheat before a thresher," Cabez stated.

Faswad flicked ash off his cigarette to the floor and glowered. "I was too late in having Russel picked up for spying on us."

He crushed out the cigarette in an ashtray, and then weighed the consequences of hurling the heavy crystal against the far wall. It would take forever to clean up, and it would only serve to make more of a mess when what he required was more order. Faswad breathed deeply and let out his tension. It was always good to think of the consequences—that's how he methodically crawled his way up the organizational maze of Hezbollah splinter politics until he reached his position.

Cabez waited until Faswad broke out of his train of thought. "Do you think Russel knew of our deal for the dozen American tanks?"

"He spotted something moving, we have no idea what for sure, and from the destruction in Pakistan, we're not sure if the tanks were even uncrated. Something destroyed everything, flattening any piece of materiel to component atoms," Cabez answered.

Faswad fired up a fresh cigarette. "And al Askari is with Russel now."

"Al Askari and another man. Dark-skinned, spoke Arabic, younger than the Americans, and athletic. They all got away in a gold-colored Toyota 4Runner."

Faswad frowned. "Watch them. If they try to roust us, we roust them. Burn them down. We can find what we need from a dead body as easily as we can from a live one."

Cabez nodded. "You're right, sir."

KALID FINALLY PULLED the 4Runner into Bolan's safehouse, and the Executioner helped Rust up the stairs. He had regained much of his strength, but the CIA man wasn't going to be running and jumping or shooting and looting in the near future. That was fine with the Executioner, who preferred to be the cat that walked by himself.

Bolan spared a glance back to Kalid, who was double-checking the streets for any signs of surveillance. His own icy blue eyes swept the perimeter and found little more than daily life. Still he didn't let down his guard. Danger signals were not going off in his brain, but that didn't mean he could relax.

"Alex, I want you to guard Rust," Bolan told him. "I need both of your heads working on figuring out what we're dealing with."

"I'd be more useful on hand, translating and interrogating," Kalid spoke up. "But I can understand. I'll be your baby-sitter."

"It's not that you're as fragile as a teacup, Alex. But you have just been through a fight, you might have a minor concussion, and you took a beating."

"You're not exactly the embodiment of health yourself," Kalid retorted. "But I'll rest up."

Bolan gave Kalid's hand a shake, then slipped into a battered old leather jacket and pulled on a motorcycle helmet. A slightly rusted, but otherwise workable Kawasaki was parked beside the Toyota. The Executioner had selected the battered, but serviceable, motorcycle because it was well designed for the narrow and uneven streets of Beirut and the back roads in the countryside. A large fiberglass storage trunk on the touring motorcycle also fit the soldier's needs. It was sized perfectly for Bolan's war bag, with its load of a rifle, grenades and spare ammo.

"You already have a target?" Kalid asked.

"Enough suspicion for a soft probe."

Kalid gave a low whistle. "Poor bastards."

"Just hold down the fort. There's some Coke in the fridge, and a machine gun propped against the sofa."

The motorcycle kicked to life. It was time to get down to business.

THE KAWASAKI RUMBLED to a halt behind a boulder and Mack Bolan turned off the engine. He still had a hike to get to the old farm equipment factory where Rust had initially spotted the Hezbollah hellions loading up the three boxcars to send to the coast. It was no secret that the factory was used by the Lebanese-based Palestinian fighters to store their rickety old T-72 tanks. Israel had visited hell upon the compound several times in the past, and Bolan could see signs of fresh reconstruction, only made possible by Lebanon suing for peace against further Israeli air force assaults.

Bolan pulled some camouflage netting across the Kawasaki and wrapped it around the vehicle, not wanting to lose his transport back to the safehouse. He paused for a moment and evaluated what he should take along, and knew that the sound-suppressed Uzi was the head weapon for this night. He wished he had more familiar hardware, but unfortunately, he hadn't been able to get his usual war bag. Instead, he had relied on the kindness of Captain Hofflower's armory. The Peshawar customized Taurus 92 was replaced with a brand-new Marine-issue Beretta M-9 pistol, complete with several 15- and 20-round magazines and a Gemtech suppressor. A .45-caliber Heckler and Koch SOCOM pistol was also given to the Executioner as his "heavy hitter." Hofflower had informed Bolan that the big .45 was loaded with MagSafe rounds—capable of punching through a windshield, but they wouldn't punch clean through a terrorist and hit a hostage if Bolan was stuck in a hostage situation. Hofflower gave the soldier a big stack of MagSafe ammo in 9 mm as well.

"If you're going to shoot a 9 mm, you might as well shoot

something that'll tear the insides up on someone," Hofflower admitted. "And this does the trick."

Bolan put the SOCOM where he normally kept his Desert Eagle and the M-9 with its 20-round magazine where his 93-R usually went. He felt almost balanced—thunder and whisper together.

There was a Robinson Armament VEPR in the Kawasaki's storage trunk. The Executioner debated overburdening himself with too much firepower when he was only moving in on a stealth assault. But he had been on too many soft probes that had gone hard, and the VEPR was made of enough polymer to make it light enough to carry as a backup to his suppressed Uzi. Besides, there was also the chance that Bolan wouldn't be able to get back to the bike. The American-built AK and its ammo would come along.

Taking to the high brush, Bolan scurried to where he could get a good view of the factory and withdrew a pair of minibinoculars. Sweeping the compound, he could tell that there was some serious activity on hand.

Mobilization, perhaps, in the wake of discovery?

Bolan went over the layout of the place, running it against the digital photographs that Rust had taken and transmitted to the Executioner. It was Rust's discovery of strange cargo that drew the Executioner in the first place. This was the first time Bolan was viewing the compound personally, and the fencing alone—two kinds of barbed wire and "flycatcher" barbs—told him all he needed to know. The perimeter was only the first part. Bolan could see a second, shorter fence, and this was on the other side of a dog run. Even now, a pair of Dobermans were racing along the channel between the two fences.

Bolan respected any guard animal.

Usually they were trained to a frenzy point through abuse and just enough malnutrition to cause blood lust, but not to impair the killing power of the predators.

It wasn't the first time Bolan would face jackals who cowered behind wolves.

Darkness descended as the soldier advanced across the scrub-and-stone-covered terrain around the perimeter fence. By the time he reached the compound, the countryside was a murky dusk. The compound's lights were slow in activating, allowing Bolan a chance to slip into their shadows before they burst into blue-white brilliance. Dropping to a crouch, he brought up the binoculars again and swept the compound. Activity was concentrated at the far end of the facility.

Bolan hoped that the constant motion and sound would draw the attention of the patrol dogs. Sweeping to his left, he realized he had no such luck as they came racing toward him. The Executioner lowered the binoculars and brought his hand to the silenced Beretta, drawing it swiftly. The sleek pistol came up to firing position in a reflexive heartbeat.

As much as the soldier hated hurting animals, the dogs would raise too much alarm. These were trained missiles of flesh, rocketing at him at nearly twenty-five miles an hour, and would slash him to ribbons the moment he tried to breach the fence. They would never allow him a moment's peace. As it was, Bolan planted his first shot in the lower jaw of the first dog. The Doberman folded over, tumbling like a soccer ball and slamming into the fence.

The fence shattered where the dog slammed into it, and the Executioner and the remaining dog were both taken off guard, turning to see tinkling chain link come apart like delicate crystal. Both soldier and guard dog returned their gazes to each other then broke for the gap in the fence. Someone had started to make a hole to get into the base themselves.

Now, the Executioner and the animal were in a race to see who would get to the hole first. Bolan tapped off single rounds at the dog, but it was moving too quickly. The Doberman leaped and twisted, and finally, it was at the hole, hopping and doing a twist in midair. With a single push of its powerful legs, it would be through the hole and at the Executioner's throat in mere heartbeats. Bolan dropped to the ground, elbows striking the dirt and he fired three fast rounds. The Doberman bounced through the hole, charging, but an explosion of crimson slowed the dog by a couple steps. Bolan triggered another round, this one striking the center of the sleek, black-furred mass, and the dog crumpled.

Bolan slipped through the fence and into the dog run, pausing to look at a piece of the chain link. It was as he'd suspected—someone had weakened the fence. With a quick scan of the area he saw a spray can under a shrub. He slipped back and picked it up.

Still full. He tried a test squirt at the branch of the plant it was under and watched as the wood and leaf whitened and snapped as a breeze blew past it.

Liquid nitrogen. It made sense—after years in the heat, suddenly supercooled metal would snap apart. Balancing the weight of the spray can in his palm, Bolan realized its owner had to be inside the compound somewhere. He squeezed through the hole in the fence again, taking the liquid nitrogen with him. It was a tight squeeze. The original user had to have had a smaller frame than Bolan.

The soldier moved to the other side of the dog run and sprayed a larger circle of brittle chain link for himself. He pushed it through, watching the fence part before him, grabbing the falling section and pulling it back through the hole before it could clatter on asphalt and alert his enemy. A quick crawl, and he was on the other side, crouched and scanning.

His brief conflict with the dogs, and the breaking of the fence hadn't sent enough sound to alert anyone at the far end of the compound. Nearby, presumably empty trailers and boxcars sat on their jacks. The Executioner kept to the shadows, crawled under a trailer and brought up his binoculars again.

A cab for an eighteen-wheeler was rolling out of a warehouse and making a crawl toward the trailers. He saw it was a Mack truck. A small smile crossed his face as he figured out the way to get closer. Turning away from the truck with his name on it, as Bolan swept the compound some more, he saw a small commotion. Two men were pulling along a woman toward a loading dock.

Focusing the binoculars tighter, he managed to make out her features. Her hair was dark, either auburn or having a tint of some red keeping it from being otherwise black. She was also compact. Not tiny and fragile, but small and toughly built, yet still maintaining a decidedly feminine form. Her eyes were covered by the checkerboard pattern of a kaffiyeh, her wrists knotted together. Even with the binoculars, he couldn't make out what language she was cursing in, but she was talking up a storm.

Bolan knew this had to have been the person who used the liquid nitrogen. She was the right size.

The Mack truck finally rolled up and made its hairpin turn to start backing into one of the trailers. Bolan knew it was now or never to try to get the woman out in one piece.

Bursting from his hiding spot, he surged forward, Beretta leading the charge this time. The driver paused, looking over and starting to cry out, but Bolan was up on the running board, gripping the door handle and shoving his suppressed Beretta through the window.

Suddenly a second, shadowy figure in the tractor-trailer's cab surged toward the Executioner, framed in the driver's window. The barrel of an AK jabbed at Bolan, the spoon-shaped muzzle brake stabbing him through his blacksuit. Instinct twisted the soldier as he slammed the butt of his pistol across the barrel. The rubber magazine floor plate smacked metal, deflecting it aside. Bolan stiff-armed the gun again. As he cut loose with the Beretta, pumping 9 mm rounds through the window, the AK went off, spitting out a blossom of heat that sizzled his skin. He cursed himself for not anticipating a shotgun rider to be literally riding shotgun. The Kalashnikov ripped off a burst, bullets tearing through the air, but cutting off as the shooter and driver both died with 9 mm bombs spreading copper shrapnel and buckshot through their heads and necks.

Stealth was gone now as the Mack continued rolling back, slamming the trailer behind it and knocking it off balance. Metal screamed and groaned, and at the other end of the compound, bodies were in motion.

Bolan hung desperately to the door, boots not jarred from the running board. He pulled the door open and let the driver's corpse slide to the ground. The Executioner reached in and hauled out the dead shotgun rider as well, grabbing the noisy AK for extra firepower.

Then, slipping behind the wheel, he rammed the big truck into Drive.

The cab was hurtling forward as fast as Bolan could rev the engine, enemy gunfire already pinging off the steel grille and punching into the safety glass.

5

Tera Geren could feel her cheek swelling where one of the Hezbollah Neanderthals had given her a crack with the butt of his rifle. She counted herself lucky that her cheekbone hadn't been snapped thanks to a generous wrapping of burlap around the butt, but with her eyes squeezed shut by a harshly tied blindfold, she could feel the bruise being aggravated. She pulled when she could get some leverage, but the two gorillas weren't going to let her go anywhere.

At least until she heard the distant, brief chatter of an AK going off. The goons holding on to her paused briefly and she managed to get her feet planted. Her hands were tied in front of her, so she knew she had that much going for her. And from her constant jostling, she felt the butt of one of the terrorist's handguns poking her in her ribs.

Just a little more distraction was all she needed.

Suddenly the air around her broke with gunfire, and she reflexively jerked out of the grip of one of the Hezbollah gunners. Almost breathless with surprise and excitement, she heard a handgun barking close to her. Somehow one of her captors managed to keep his hand on his weapon and her at the same time.

It didn't matter. Geren had her feet planted wide, giving her the extra leverage to resist his pull. She popped loose and moved toward where she heard the other gunman, grabbing where she figured his belt would be. Fingers raked cloth until they snagged his waistband, and she grabbed on tight, swinging her body with all her might, pivoting. There was a cry of dismay, then the head-banging crack of close-range handgun fire thundering at her.

Nothing hit, though. Bullets went wide after a sickly impact jerked the form in her grasp. The guy she grabbed wailed in Arabic at the insanity of the shooter. Geren cut him off with a sharp shoulder-butt to his back, and then reached up, tearing away the blindfold.

People all around were reacting in a mixed storm of fury and panic, and her captor was torn between shooting an unarmed woman and reacting to the headlights of a truck barreling down on them. Geren took advantage of that moment of indecision to pluck the side arm from the injured man and kick the back of his knee to send him tumbling away from his dropped long arm.

The Hezbollah man had carried a Glock, and she hoped that it had a live round in the chamber, or else her escape attempt was going to be pretty damn short. She brought up the gun as the hardguy suddenly realized the equation was changing.

Geren pulled the trigger and caught the terrorist between a Mack truck, a 9 mm slug and four of its closest friends. The line of bullets she punched into the terrorist spun him lifelessly away, and she crouched low, swinging the barrel in an arc as she backed away from the path of the truck. The big vehicle swerved away from her, but swung around, smashing into bodies as they got in the driver's path. The truck swerved hard and fishtailed, an awesome roaring sound ripping through the air during the maneuver.

The door on the passenger side flew open, the driver glaring at her.

"Get in!"

English. Not an instant guarantee of him being a good guy,

but considering how many dazed and confused Hezbollah gunmen were around her, she'd take a gamble that he wasn't interested in punching a good Israeli girl's ticket. She reached up, ditching the Glock into the seat well of the truck so she could grab a handhold and yank herself into the vehicle. As soon as she got a good hold, the truck started moving again, tires squealing and air brakes shrieking. A bullet bounced off the running board just below her booted foot as she finally yanked herself inside, curling up and pivoting on the seat.

She caught the flash of mirrored steel as she started to seat herself, and hesitated. A microsecond later, recognition kicked in and she held out her bound wrists, feeling the sharp blade slash through her bonds. Hands freed, she grabbed a handle on the dashboard, leaned out and yanked the door shut just moments before a peppering rain of bullets crashed into it.

"Have they moved anything out yet?" the driver asked, pumping the gas and turning the wheel, accelerating.

"Four oversized cargo containers," Geren answered immediately. "I saw that much."

"Uzi or AK?" the man asked.

Geren grabbed at the Uzi and hauled it across the space between them, twisting to the window. Outside the spider-webbed morass of broken glass that used to be a windshield, she could see small lights flickering and big lights blazing.

"Watch your eyes!"

"Blow it," the driver agreed.

Geren hammered off a half magazine, 9 mm rounds smashing fist-sized holes in the broken glass, allowing them to see better as more and more broken diamonds rained inside and outside the cab.

Now the big man behind the wheel could see buildings. He swerved to avoid one warehouse, the truck bucking as it crunched its way over more bodies.

"I hope you know how to drive a car better than this."

"It's been a while since I've driven a truck this size, and in such tight maneuvering quarters," the stranger admitted.

"Roll on," Geren answered, squirting a short burst from her Uzi into a group of gunners.

The gearshift snarled and bellowed like a wounded beast as the brawny arm of the driver worked it. She took a look across the dashboard. "Something wrong?" Geren asked.

"We took hits to the gas tanks. We'll run out of gas in a bit, but I'm more worried about them sparking and setting a fire after us."

Geren looked in the mirror and spotted men racing into the wake of the truck, shooting at the ground. One man screamed as a bouncing bullet leaped back into his gut, but sparks flew from the impacts. Flames licked to life.

"They just figured that out too," she answered. "I need a fresh magazine."

"Grab the Glock," the driver admonished. "We're not sticking around here."

He swung the wheel, aiming for the loading dock that Geren had been watching all day, oblivious to the two trucks trying to get out of the way.

BOLAN GUNNED THE TRUCK toward the loading dock, counting on the relatively low velocity of the two enemy trucks to work in his favor. He glanced to see the Uzi-packing woman strapping on her seat belt at the last second. Bolan had his blade jammed into the side of the seat, ready to slash open his and her seat belts should they get stuck.

At just under thirty miles per hour, the truck cab, stained with blood and gore, clipped one advancing truck, tearing off its bumper before hitting the second truck at an angle. The driver screamed in horror as his cab was suddenly whipped around sideways, velocity bleeding off as metal mangled metal. Bolan felt a sledgehammer smash into his chest where the seat belt caught him, and he spit blood from where he bit into his lip. His head was swimming, and he didn't even have the manual dexterity to grope at the seat-belt release latch. Instead, he shoved on the nylon strap, brought up his knife and sliced. The strap parted, and the automatic winding winch for the belt slurped it out of his way like a piece of black fettuccine. He looked to the woman who simply clenched her hand on her seat-belt release. She had never let go of the thing before impact and surged forward, scooping up both the Uzi and the Glock as quick as she could.

Bolan appreciated her preparedness and brought up the AK, swinging it butt-first through what little remained of the windshield, opening an exit to escape from. In the bullet cracked side mirror, he caught a flash of light as flames leaped up from where the burning line of fuel caught up with the truck. Fortunately, diesel was not as explosive as gasoline, and they still had time to get free.

"Go!" Bolan ordered.

The woman slid down the hood of the truck in a blur, and Bolan was right after her, leaping off the hood of the doomed vehicle. In the alcove formed by the three trucks, they paused for a moment, regathering their senses.

"What do I call you?"

"Tera. Tera Geren," she answered. "And you are?"

"Brandon Stone. Get up there, Tera." He waved her at the stairs leading up into the loading dock. She didn't waste a single moment, hotfooting it up the steps with the Executioner in pursuit. Flames leaped higher on the truck they'd just left. Geren dived to the ground as a wild burst sparked off the steel pipe railing of the stairwell.

Bolan spun and saw that the shotgun rider for the truck they only barely clipped was still struggling to get out of the cab and aim his AK one-handed. Bracing his own weapon with both hands, the Executioner taught the gunman a lesson in proper weapon handling. Unfortunately, the lesson in marksmanship was wasted as the Hezbollah murderer was slammed messily into the door of the cab, his torso blown to chunks by Bolan's stream of 7.62 mm ComBloc rounds. He glanced back to Geren, who was cursing as she clutched her side.

Bolan moved to her, hooking her arm and carrying her through the loading dock door just as the diesel fire flared hotter. "Where are you hit?"

"It's a nick," she muttered. "Doesn't matter."

Bolan swept the interior of the warehouse, spotting no motion, and then took a closer look at the gunshot. She was right, the bullet only creased the skin along her rib cage. The rut of flesh was only a fingertip deep and ran a couple inches, but it bled a lot. "Can you breathe okay?"

"I'm fine," Geren replied.

Bolan stuffed a couple of Uzi magazines into the woman's hands and nodded to her. "I'll apply a quick field dressing. You reload and keep an eye out."

"You don't mess…" she stopped, wincing as Bolan ripped her damaged BDU blouse wider to apply the dressing. "You don't mess around."

The soldier took a pad of sterile gauze and attached it to the underside of two parallel strips of duct tape, pressing it gently, but firmly to her skin. "That'll control the bleeding for now, but you might need some stitches," he said.

"We'll live that long?" she asked.

Bolan switched his AK for the VEPR, handing the heavier weapon to Geren. "I've been in worse spots."

Before she could answer, the flare of a flash fire glowed hotly through the open loading dock gate. The soldier instinctively shielded the woman from the glare, and then gave her a gentle shove deeper into the warehouse.

"They're not going to get though that inferno. They also probably won't want to try any of the doors on that side of the building, in case the fire spreads," Bolan explained.

As if on cue, the door kicked in on an emergency exit at the other end of the warehouse. Three men charged in at full speed, but Bolan brought up his VEPR, punching out two bursts into the closest gunners. Geren's AK was up and tracking, ripping a chain saw of rounds across the belly of the third. The trio tumbled, weapons dropping.

"Look, they gave us fresh ammo," Geren said with a mock grin.

"Let's not let it go to waste." Bolan crossed the distance to the downed gunners in a few easy, loping strides and dropped to one knee, pulling guns from lifeless hands and handing Geren spare AK magazines for her recent acquisition.

"I like you, Brandon. We might live long enough to exchange phone numbers," she said, keeping the chatter going. Bolan had seen the defense mechanism before.

Bolan caught her smile before he continued scanning the warehouse, especially the entrance the terrorists came through. More would be coming, but they might be spreading out, trying some of the other entrances. He looked up and spotted catwalks. A good place for them to command the scene, but there'd be damned little means of escape up there.

Unless…

Bolan followed one catwalk visually, spotting a path to a bank of windows. "Come on," he said.

More doors burst open, and Bolan let Geren go ahead, spinning the VEPR's muzzle and laying down the remainder of his first magazine into the gunners who came through the closest door. Bodies crashed and tumbled, some dead, some in retreat, seeking cover. At the far door, intermittent fire crackled, but nobody seemed interested in making themselves targets by moving into position to actually hit the

Executioner. Geren, on the stairway, tapped off a couple short bursts to keep heads down while Bolan reloaded.

The Executioner wasn't expecting to take out all their pursuers, but every head ducked was a trigger finger not spitting steel-cored rounds. He returned a series of short, but withering bursts at the gunners crouched behind crates and barrels.

"Where now?" Geren asked.

Bolan pointed to the window. "Take out the glass."

"Lend me your .45. I'm not wasting rifle ammo on that job," she said.

Bolan unleathered the big German pistol. Despite the small size of the woman, her hands managed to wrap around the grip. She still needed both hands to properly grip the pistol as she was just a shade over five feet, but she handled the thundering recoil of the SOCOM as she blasted off the entire magazine, smashing glass to shards and splinters. The gunners inside the warehouse screamed as debris rained on them. One man, distracted by being cut in the rain of glass, stepped out into the open.

Bolan blew his skull apart with a precision burst.

Terrorists were frantic after seeing their friend decapitated. One opened fire and burned off the ammo in his weapon, screaming to high heaven. Two more gunners crouched down tighter and out of sight, avoiding the mad moments of their buddy's panic fire. As the panicked gunner ran out of ammo, Bolan sighted on him and gave him a short burst that ripped him open, breastbone to throat, dropping him backward.

Bolan could make out shouting below and heard the Arabic words for "Get out!"

Geren glanced back at him. "They're getting ready to try something."

"I figured that," Bolan said. He pulled his knife and took

back his Uzi, slashing the sling on the weapon in two long strips of nylon. "Take this."

"What are... You're kidding."

"No. I don't kid," Bolan said. He charged along the catwalk, and Geren was right on his heels. The Hezbollah gunmen were already in retreat as casks of flaming gasoline were thrown through the doors of the warehouse.

The bottles burst, spilling burning fuel in cones and waves of flashing flame, wood taking to light instantly. There wouldn't be much time for the Executioner and his new ally to get to safety. They were high in the rafters, where deadly smoke would immediately begin accumulating. On the floor of the warehouse, they would have stood a better chance, but only until the fire reached them, or they ran right into the blazing guns of the terrorists.

Reaching the window, Bolan crouched, keeping to shadow. Geren lit beside him, looking out.

Nobody was looking up at the window that had been blown out. He scanned around and looked to see if there were any power lines attached. He'd spotted some kind of lines and cords on other buildings. Bolan saw one, coming down from the corner, but first they'd have to get onto the roof to get to it.

"How are you at heights?" Bolan asked softly.

She looked down. "Where are we going?"

"I'm going to boost you to the roof, so you can get to the power line."

"We'll be exposed for all the time it takes to climb up there."

"I'll cover you, if you think you can make the climb," Bolan said.

Geren looked back into the swirling clouds of toxic, choking smoke. "I'll flap my arms if I have to. Gimme the boost."

With the grace of a gymnast, she bounded off Bolan's

clasped hands and leaped up, grabbing the corner of the roof.
She pulled herself, Bolan continuing to push up and give her
some assistance. The short woman had little difficulty getting up on top of the warehouse with something to push her
feet against. The Executioner's mind raced as he figured out
what he could do to achieve the same.

Suddenly Geren's arm and tiny hand reached down over
the edge. He heard her issue a terse "C'mon!"

Bolan reached up and grabbed her hand, using his other
hand to grab hold of the top of the window frame. He glanced
back down, and thankfully, nobody could see them. He could
barely see through the black smoke pouring past him. He
didn't know how exposed he was, and maybe the enemy
could see his feet dangling out of the cloud of smoke, but he
doubted it. They certainly would have opened fire if they had
noticed him.

He cast aside his doubts and dug his boot into the window frame long enough to pull hard on Geren's arm and
shove himself up with the power of his right leg to grab at
the corner of the building. He released Geren's hand and
threw his other arm up higher, feeling his own weight crushing his armpit. He winced in pain as the Beretta was trapped
between unyielding aluminum and his ribs. Geren grabbed
Bolan by his shoulders and pulled, his foot giving one last
kick against the side of the building, getting him rolling flat
onto the roof, out of breath, covered in a new layer of bruises
and pulled-muscle pain.

"That's the path of least resistance," Geren remarked,
pointing to the guy wire going to ground level. "It's a steel
cable with utility wires leading to the top. There's an access
stairwell to the roof too, but we'd be sitting ducks."

Bolan sat up, his breath regained. "Give me a moment to
arrange my distraction, get to the cable."

Geren moved over, and the Executioner removed a quartet of munitions from his battle harness, thumbing the cotter pins on the grenades straight. With the first two, he popped the pins with a sharp thumb jerk, then threw the grenades over the far edge of the roof. Even as they went sailing, Bolan's thumbs again snapped out the pins on the second two grenades in quick succession, and then he was up and moving for the corner of the roof. The first explosion flashed on the other side, and he unfurled his length of Uzi sling.

Geren wrapped her strap around the cable and pushed off, shooting down the diagonal as quickly as possible, sailing to ground level and the fence as if she were rocket powered. Bolan leaped and snagged the cable with his own piece of sling, burning along as well. He took a glance up and saw that his weight on the nylon band was shredding it against the tearing surface of the steel cable. He looked down and saw he had a twelve-foot drop to go, right behind a pair of Hezbollah gunmen who were backing away from the burning warehouse.

Bolan released his strap and dropped, knees bending to cushion his fall. The impact of his fall alerted the two gunmen, and they began to turn, weapons slowly tracking around to see what was behind them. The Executioner fired off a crushing kidney punch that caught the man on the left in a web of paralyzing agony. The second terrorist started to cry out in anger and warning, but Bolan swung a right-handed hammer blow that slammed the gunman right in his solar plexus. The breath paralyzed in his chest, the second gunner tried to squeak out a warning to his fellow fighters, but Bolan got out his knife and finished off the breathless killer with a wicked slash across his throat. The first man was still squirming in muted agony, and Bolan brought down the knife into his heart, cracking the gunner's breastbone and killing him instantly.

The Executioner pulled his knife free and wiped the blade on the uniform of the dead man, then looked around.

Geren was missing, and the Executioner wondered what had happened to the woman until he saw a Nissan pickup truck drive toward him, its headlights out.

The truck rolled to a halt, and a pretty, full-lipped face poked out from the shadows of the cab. "Hey, Brandon. Is a Nissan okay with you, or should I find a more macho truck?"

Bolan gave her a pat on the arm and clambered into the cargo bed of the pickup. "Get moving."

Geren chuckled and gunned the engine, headlights suddenly blazing to life as she tore off at high speed. "I spotted this thing while we were on the roof."

Bolan looked up and saw the chain-link fence was close. Hezbollah gunmen were opening fire with their rifles, trying to cut off the Nissan. But the gunmen hadn't counted on return fire from the dashboard of the Nissan, where Geren was jamming her rifle through a hole in the safety glass and triggering long bursts.

Gunfire dinged against the tailgate of the pickup, and more trucks were rolling toward them. The Executioner reloaded his VEPR, shouldered it and put a long burst across the windshield of the nearest truck as it and its crew of gunmen got within thirty feet. The windshield disappeared in a spray of blood-spattered glass. The driver himself was slumped over, dead. Bolan felt the Nissan's right fender peel away as Geren deflected slightly off the gate of the compound, more bullets whizzing overhead in a hornet storm.

"You okay up there?" Bolan asked.

"I'll live!" Geren shouted.

The driverless pickup slammed through chain link, toppling over onto one of the gate guards who had survived Geren's initial hell sweep. Pulped gunmen were strewed around the gate, and a second pickup truck was just moments too late on the brake to stop from smashing the first vehicle and its hapless crew even further.

The Executioner and the woman tore off into the night, pursuit long behind them.

6

When the battered and smashed Nissan pickup pulled up to the safehouse, Alex Kalid was waiting at the door, weapon at his side. He didn't recognize the vehicle, but he knew the earmarks of the man who would be driving it up here. Sure enough, it was Striker, the big man covered in sweat, dirt and more than a little blood.

With him was a petite, if determined, woman behind the wheel. Her green eyes flashed vibrantly in the spill of light from the safehouse's back door, doubly so when she made out his features.

"He's with me," Bolan said to her. "Alex Johnson, meet Tera Geren."

Kalid managed a smile. "Pleasure's all mine."

"Johnson. That's not an Egyptian name," she spoke up, stepping out of the truck's cab. She walked past him, and Kalid felt the chill.

"That's because I'm American born. And from your accent, so are you."

Geren was taken aback by his comment, and Kalid smirked. "You have an almost accent. Urban U.S., but just a bit of imperceptible twang, like you come from a western state."

"Like that bit of Hispanic lilt in your voice?" she prodded.

"You're good. I thought I dropped that long ago."

Bolan interrupted. "Is Russel all right?"

"He's doing better," Kalid answered. "You get anything?"

"Her," Bolan mentioned with a nod of his head toward Geren.

"Yeah, but can we pound information out of her like we could a Hezbollah member?" Kalid replied. "Unless…"

"Try it, buster," Geren answered. She was over a foot shorter than he was, but she seemed to get bigger as she glared at him. Then she grinned, knowing it was a joke.

Bolan clapped Kalid on the shoulder. "We could try being nice."

"Okay, but I'll keep the whips and chains handy," Kalid quipped.

The trio made its way into the safehouse to find Rust, a cold pack resting on the table at his elbow, looking at a sheaf of notes in his hand. He barely glanced up at the entrance of the group.

"Looks like you're burning the midnight oil," Bolan told Rust.

The CIA man looked up and grimaced. "Smells like you've been swimming in it."

"The bad guys tried to cook us like rats," Bolan answered. "What have you got?"

"I've got about eighty pages of notes over the past six months just on Hezbollah hobnobbing with arms dealers," Rust replied. "They've been trying to buy some stuff, as usual, but for the first time, they seemed to have something to sell."

"Sell. As in U.S.-built tanks leased to Egypt?" the Executioner prodded.

"U.S.-built tanks?" Kalid asked, feeling his blood run cold.

"First generation M1 Abrams," Bolan pointed out. "The same kind that hit Nitzala and killed hundreds of people."

Kalid winced, and then recovered his composure. He looked at Geren's face, but it was a poker mask. She wasn't going to reveal anything. "So now we know what we're up against," he said.

"No, we don't. The Hezbollah is just acting as a middle-man. They received a shipment of something, and they're selling off a fraction to make a profit," Bolan explained. "Pure profit."

"That's a pretty long jump to make that conclusion, big man," Geren spoke up. "How do you know?"

"Because I don't see the Hezbollah dropping three hundred million dollars on tanks, and only using seventy-five million worth to smash a small town to pieces unless it was a gift from someone else," Bolan growled. "You didn't happen to see Faswad at the compound, did you?"

It took a moment for the woman to respond to Bolan's pointed inquiry. "I was blindfolded."

"Before they blindfolded you. I'm sure you didn't just go in with a can of liquid nitrogen and no binoculars. Or better yet, a digital camera."

She looked at Bolan, then down as the Executioner held out his hand, palm up. "It's probably on a flash memory card."

Geren inhaled deeply and reached into her waistband. She came up with a pair of blue-and-white plastic cards.

"I palmed them and replaced one with a blank. How did you know?" she asked.

"You had the mind-set to take out one of your guards while blindfolded. Slipping the memory on your digital camera and replacing it with a blank card would be nothing for someone who thinks like you," Bolan answered.

Geren shrugged.

"We did change the terrain, the wide loads did drive away and Faswad wasn't at the compound for more than a minute," Geren said.

Kalid could feel a rush of frustration radiate off Bolan. "Just missed him again?"

"It's only the first time I went after him," Bolan said. "And I'm still on the prowl. Any more intel, Tera?"

"I don't even know who you are," she replied, "except for the fact that this guy is a freakish mix of Cuban and Egyptian, that guy's a wool-dyed CIA spook, and you…"

Their eyes locked hard.

"I'm someone not used to playing politics and stroking egos," Bolan stated.

Geren blinked but didn't flinch. "No. You're not. And that's why you happen to have three-hour-old data in your hand."

"Welcome to the team," Bolan said, holding out his hand.

Kalid sighed with relief when she took it.

IMAL FASWAD FELT A CHILL run through him as he heard the radio reports of death and devastation at the compound.

"Turn that off," he grumbled.

Cabez nodded to one of his underlings and the radio clicked off with the abruptness of a gunshot.

"Al Askari lives up to his reputation," Cabez said.

"I knew I should have brought the girl along instead of leaving her there." Faswad cursed himself and looked sideways to Cabez. "What did she have in her camera?"

"It was empty. She hadn't taken any pictures, or she purged the memory," Cabez explained, holding out the camera.

Faswad examined the device for a moment. "It has a removable flash memory card."

Cabez blinked.

"She switched out whatever useful information she got for a blank chip."

"Well, our men will find it on her," Cabez said.

Faswad shook his head. "Two people escaped from the compound. One was a woman."

"It might not have been her," Cabez tried to explain.

"Of course not. It was James Bond and one of his beautiful assistants, perhaps Halle Berry, no?"

Cabez hit the floor, his cheek stinging. Faswad rubbed his sore palm and then slipped his hands into his pockets.

"No need to get sarcastic," Cabez said, slowly getting up. Off balance, he wasn't able to dodge the tip of Faswad's boot smashing into his shin, knocking him sprawling onto his face, the carpet ripping his cheek and chin raw.

Since the fool was bald, Faswad bent over and dug his fingers into Cabez's collar and yanked him upright. Jerked to his feet, and beyond, Cabez kicked empty air before he was dropped, staggering against the wall.

"Kazan is still ready to move with his tanks?" Faswad asked.

Cabez nodded, his eyes lit with the terror of a panicked animal.

"Then get out of my sight, you bloody fool. I'm sick of you!"

Cabez spun and got out of the room.

It was going to be one of those nights, Faswad knew. He went to his desk and pulled out a Browning Hi-Power, checked its load and slipped it into his waistband.

Whatever storm was coming was going to be greeted by lightning and thunder.

THE EXECUTIONER LOWERED the M-16 and let out his breath. His finger relaxed on the trigger, and he looked left and right. Alex Kalid and Tera Geren were with him, in the shadows of an empty apartment, looking across the street toward Imal Faswad in his protected home. The building they were in had seen better decades, the balcony having long since been shorn away by constant shock waves from shelling.

The Hezbollah commander made no secret of his hideout, and no bones about the fact that he was well protected. Bolan didn't think that his M-16 could penetrate the mesh that covered the terrorist's window anyway. He didn't think anything short of a .50-caliber weapon or a rocket launcher could have cut through it. Faswad had a breeze, even if it did have to whisper through impenetrable steel mesh.

Geren looked at him as if to ask why he didn't take the shot to remove Faswad, the moment he was alone. She didn't say it out loud; they were just a dozen yards from Faswad's apartment complex.

Bolan sequenced the MP3 player hooked to his M-16's snooper microphone, then handed her the earpiece. He played the mention of Kazan and the tanks. Geren's face darkened for a moment.

At the door to the apartment, Kalid did his best pigeon coo.

Bolan and Geren clung to the shadows, staying still as the blazing spill of a flashlight swept through the hall. The guard passed, and the Executioner relaxed again, looking out the window.

"He was talking about someone with tanks, wasn't he?" Bolan whispered to Geren.

She nodded. "Faswad asked if someone named Kazan was ready to move with his tanks."

"So that means someone else is going to get attacked. We have to get to Faswad."

"Or we can listen in on his communications," Kalid suggested. "That guard obviously has something to get his orders from."

Bolan weighed his options for a moment.

Getting into the abandoned apartment building had taken some stealth, and so far they had avoided sending any more terrorists out of this world. The Executioner was here for intel, not for a clean sweep, and any enemy contact drastically increased the odds that the bad guys would shut up and let their guns do the talking instead.

"Quick and quiet."

Kalid's smile gleamed in the dark. "I'll just give our friend a gold star."

Geren looked confused as the ex-blacksuit slipped into the corridor.

Bolan returned to his crouch near the window, still keeping to the shadows.

Below, in the street, cars were arranged so that they provided a maze against anyone who would try to drive up to the front door. Unless they had a tank of their own, there was no way to rapidly pull up or maneuver down this street. The Hezbollah had learned that suicide bombs could take them as well as their enemies.

Car bombs weren't the Executioner's weapon of choice. There was too much of a chance of hitting a stray passerby with the backwash of an explosion. Cleansing flame was not meant for civilians to suffer. His war was with those who considered a bystander killed to be an acceptable loss. While he knew that as long as there was war, there would be civilian casualties, deep within his own warrior's heart, he vowed never to add another to that fire.

He scanned the building some more, trying to figure out how to make his strike with what he had and with a minimum of loss. Bolan knew that he was going to be leaving at least Geren behind under the pretense of supplying cover fire, and he was also contemplating doing the same for Kalid.

The Executioner was a realist, knowing he couldn't fight the entire world by himself, but he was also a man loath to let harm befall anyone else on his crusade. He'd been one man, fighting against the odds for so long, that the prospect of going alone against an entire complex full of Hezbollah guards and terrorists didn't make him flinch.

He did flinch from the mental image of Kalid and Geren, their chests ripped apart by gunfire, bodies flopping to the floor in pools of their own blood.

Too many beloved friends had met the same fate.

Bolan set his jaw and tore himself from his reverie. It was time for work.

Time to do his job and stop some madmen from sending a squadron of tanks to destroy some helpless settlement.

Shadows moved among the maze of cars below, catching his attention. Bolan snapped the M-16 to his shoulder, peering through its 4x scope. Shadows, in black, armed with suppressed Uzi submachine guns.

Bolan gave Geren a tap and she looked down, seeing them as well. She studied them quickly through the scope on her own VEPR rifle. "They're not ours. We don't use Uzis for black ops."

"I figured as much," Bolan answered. "Someone is looking to take out Faswad and make it look like the Israelis."

"To cover up their own dirty deeds?" Geren asked.

Bolan nodded. He wanted to call out to Kalid to tell him to forget the sentry. They had a chance to take a prisoner from the conspirators involved in the tank trading. However, making a noise would betray the fact that Kalid was on the prowl, it might even get the young fighting man killed.

He glanced back down and saw a guard crucified by inaudible spurts of gunfire, a second one tumbling lifelessly at the door to the apartment building.

The strangers in black were moving in.

Then the gunfire in the hall erupted.

ALESSANDRO KALID NEVER believed he had the secrets of ninja invisibility, despite the quartet of throwing stars wrapped around his forearms. After all, ninja movies were as realistic as action movies. He paused to restrain a smile, remembering exactly who he was teaming with.

Okay, maybe some people lived the impossible and implausible every day through sheer force of will. But Kalid wasn't fooling himself with the concept of being an invisible, noiseless, mystical ninja capable of killing a man with a single tap of his finger. He did, however, understand the principles of stealth intimately.

Unlike the sentry, who produced enough sound to alert the cockroaches in the next building. Kalid moved in conjunction with the guy's foot stomps and belabored breathing as he sucked on a cigarette to calm jittery nerves. The disgusting slurping and wheezing of his enjoyment of the cigarette reminded Kalid of why he had given up the filthy habit after only a few months.

The sentry stopped, and Kalid paused, keeping beyond the sloppy halo of luminescence from his flashlight. He took a quick glance over his shoulder, to make sure nobody else was around, and that movement saved his life. In the darkness, he would have never seen the ribbon of steel lashing like lightning at his throat. The knife glinted off the reflected flashlight glow, however, and Kalid dropped to the ground, steel embedding in drywall where his throat was moments ago.

He snapped out a hard kick to the mass hidden in the shadows, foot striking thigh and causing a grunt to explode from the throat of the would-be killer. Suddenly something dropped behind him, and Kalid was immersed in light, seeing his antagonist. A man in black was armed with a sound-suppressed Uzi that he was scrambling to pull up on its sling and fire.

Enough of that. Kalid lunged, hands outstretched, grasping the Uzi and forcing all his weight on it. The enemy gunman struggled to maneuver his weapon as Kalid shoved the weapon between them. The Uzi slammed into soft flesh and clunked hard against pelvic bone and hard pouches on the gunman's belt. The impact set off the submachine gun, quiet rounds ripping off in its muted roar. The impact of the bullets on drywall was louder, and the cone of light from the flashlight clouded with splinters, dust and debris.

Kalid pushed forward, going down to his knees and ducking low as another struggle sounded behind him. He didn't want to make a large target for whatever gun muzzle was at his back. So far, it was a three-way fight, and two sides were set to kill anyone who got in their way.

Kalid and his opponent slammed into the floor with a hard thud, and the guy beneath him screamed as the muzzle-blast from his weapon scorched his hip. The Uzi finally locked empty, and with a surge of energy Kalid pushed up onto one hand and brought his elbow down with crushing force between the newcomer's legs. Another blistering howl of pain split the air and in Egyptian-accented Arabic, a voice cried out behind him.

"Zimal! Are you—"

"Don't shoot!" Kalid answered quickly, praying he had every inflection of his father's Egyptian accent.

The other gunman froze for a moment, and Kalid rolled out of the way, ripping the P-226 from its thigh holster.

The Egyptian gunman brought up his weapon, trying to track him as he disappeared into the shadows beyond the spill of the flashlight. Kalid was able to see where he was by the muted red glow of his suppressed weapon, the muzzle-flash dimmed, but not dismissed, as the brutal burns on Zimal's hip attested to. Kalid locked the glowing nightsights of his pistol just above the flickering muzzle-flash and fired as fast and hard as he could. The SIG-Sauer created a flashing thunderstorm in the confines of the hallway, muzzle-blast overpressure hammering his head.

The Uzi-packing Egyptian, however, was suffering more than a headache from the noise. His chest, slammed by 9 mm slugs, puffed out spurts of blood that misted in the glare of the flashlight. Kalid's target went down, groaning and clutching at wounds.

Zimal, however, picked up his second wind and tried to

grab Kalid's wrist. The ex-blacksuit flipped his pistol across his chest, not wanting to get his own muzzle rammed into his belly. The mysterious Egyptian commando pulled on Kalid's arm, trying to break it since he couldn't pry the gun loose. Kalid instead twisted his arm and brought his other hand, filled with the steel of the SIG-Sauer, hard into Zimal's face.

Flesh tore and blood flew from the impact. Kalid hauled back and brought his gun down again, feeling bone crush as more flesh pulped. He stopped counting the impacts after ten, prying his trapped wrist free and using both hands to keep bringing down the handgun to continue to crush the head of the guy who tried to kill him.

"Alex!" a voice cut through his haze.

He looked up, and Bolan stepped into the light, concern softening his hawkish features.

"Are you okay?"

"Sorry about the noise," Kalid said. He stuffed the bloody pistol into his hip holster and grabbed for his shoulder-slung rifle. "They're Egyptian. I heard one speak."

"And they're moving on Faswad."

Kalid bent and pulled a pistol off the Egyptian he'd beaten to death. Unleathering the P-226, he placed his adversary's pistol in the holster and stuffed the SIG-Sauer into his butt pack. He didn't want to have to use the handgun until he checked it for damage from multiple impacts with a human skull.

"Then we'd better get to Faswad first," Kalid surmised.

"That's the plan, Alex," Bolan answered.

Kalid was hot on the big man's heels.

7

Major Pedal Tofo heard the gunfire in the abandoned apartment building behind him as he was storming through the entrance of Imal Faswad's building. Gripping his Uzi tighter, he cursed Zimal and Orund for allowing someone to get off gunshots to raise alarm. He'd personally break the fingers of their left hands for this.

He and the rest of the cleanup crew were going to have to make do with what little surprise that they had managed. The lobby of the apartment building was filled with Hezbollah agents who had been trying to relax despite a palpable edge of fear in the air. At the sight of six shadowy wraiths entering, packing automatic weapons, the terrorists froze in disbelief. Tofo held down the trigger of his Uzi, sweeping his sixth of the room. The other members of the Egyptian commando team were cutting the room into slices, hammering muffled Parabellum slugs into whoever they saw. It was a simultaneous sweep as the eight clueless terrorists were just too slow to get a good grip on their stashed weaponry.

The lobby was easy.

Tofo was going to have to work for everything else.

He turned to his men. Two were to take the elevator, while he and the rest were going to hoof it up the main stairs, dealing with any resistance along the way. With audacity and violence of action, the two men sent ahead would be able to form an anvil against which any resistance would be smashed.

With the team split further, Tofo led the charge up the stairs, immediately spotting a half-dressed Hezbollah gunman stumbling onto the stairs, rifle held at waist level. Tofo's Uzi chattered mutedly and ripped open the gunner. Without a second thought, the major sidestepped the corpse and continued upward, one of his commandos kneeling on the landing behind him and opening fire into a hallway.

Autofire finally erupted in full throaty volume in the quiet apartment complex, and Tofo took the stairs three at a time. His black BDUs were soaked with sweat as he continued upward at a breakneck pace. A grenade thundered below him, and Tofo knew his commandos were in for a fight.

The Egyptian major was a professional. Slamming against a wall, he looked up and spotted a trio of gunners scrambling to take up a defensive position at the top of the stairs. One of them screamed as he was stitched from behind, and Tofo swept the other two with his submachine gun.

He looked down, and saw all three of his men coming up, only one man showing signs of slowing down with a gunshot wound drenching his pant leg with dark, sticky blood.

"Hold the stairwell," Tofo ordered him, handing him a couple spare fragmentation grenades. The Egyptian commando, Anwar, nodded. Tofo recognized the sweat glistening on his face as a sign of shock and blood loss, but surrounded by enemies, there was no way they could stop to give him even minor medical assistance. He continued into the depths of the hallway for his date with Faswad.

THE EXECUTIONER HAD crossed the street and reached the dead Hezbollah guards at the entrance to the apartment building when he heard the first grenade explode and automatic weapons hammering incessantly inside. Faswad had a hardsite here, but the men striking into the depths of a terrorist head shed were consummate professionals. Entering the lobby, he saw it was filled with dead bodies, but the destruction from autofire was minimal. The intruders could aim swiftly, and put their lead on target with precision and lightning quickness.

Trained commandos, dressed in black, hitting an enemy so hard they didn't even have time to react. It would have given Mack Bolan pause if he weren't in a rush to rescue Imal Faswad. He'd started for the stairs when a couple of gunners appeared from the back of the lobby, brandishing a handgun and a rifle, a look of confusion on each face. Bolan paused in midstep, bringing around his M-16 and triggering a short burst that took out the rifleman. Two VEPR rifles blasted simultaneously from the entrance as Geren and Kalid opened fire on the handgunner, blowing him into so much stew meat.

"Stay here and guard the lobby. Don't engage the Hezbollah agents if you don't have to, but watch out for the guys in black. They're hard core," Bolan told them.

Bolan could tell that Alex Kalid was ready to follow him to the gates of Hades armed with a spoon if the Executioner only gave the word, and was frustrated to be relegated to rear security. The look of frustration disappeared after only a heartbeat, however.

"Stay hard!" Kalid called out.

Geren and Kalid separated to take cover and Bolan turned, continuing up the stairs, finding the corpse of a gunman ahead of him. He looked at the landing, smoke billowing yet from that first grenade detonation. He looked into a hallway and saw a group of armed men and women, cut down by autofire. Distantly, he could hear the cries of frightened children. A head poked around the corner, holding a weapon, looking at the Executioner.

The soldier checked his fire, seeing a teenaged girl, armed

with a pistol, peering with bloodshot, tear-filled eyes. This was a full-fledged homestead, as Bolan had feared it would be. The Egyptian commandos were here to make sure Faswad and anyone in the same building would never speak again.

A roaring gun battle sounded a couple floors above, the thunder spilling down the stairs in a waterfall of noise.

Bolan put his finger to his lips and waved the girl back behind cover.

Saving Faswad was one thing, but there were innocent lives at stake. He spun and raced down the steps back to the lobby.

"Tera, Alex. We have noncombatants penned in on the second floor at least," Bolan said.

"Noncombatants here?" Geren asked.

"Children, Tera," Bolan snarled.

"Oh, damn," she answered.

"I saw at least one kid armed. Be careful, and try not to hurt anyone," Bolan ordered.

"You make it sound so easy," Kalid quipped.

"If I were interested in easy work, I wouldn't be here. Move it!"

SURE, GEREN THOUGHT AS she ascended the stairs to the second floor, Alex "Johnson" on her heels. Brandon could go storming into a firefight where he could shoot anyone he damn well pleased, but he left them to the no-shoot scenarios.

"I presume you speak Arabic," Kalid said to her as he braced himself in the hallway.

"Yeah. I find it a useful job skill for when I travel to nations full of Arab people plotting to kill Israelis," she responded.

"These are kids," Kalid told her. "They're too young to plot."

"You've never seen a seventeen-year-old with a bomb strapped to her belly take out a schoolyard before," Geren responded.

Kalid froze, then turned toward her. "We can discuss the politics of your handling of the Palestinian peace accord after we are away from people trying to kill us, all right? Until then, speak only when spoken to."

"Yassah massah," Geren mocked.

Kalid looked as if he were a few steps from a major cerebral hemorrhage. Geren smirked at this minor victory.

"We come in peace!" Kalid called out in Arabic. "You can keep your weapons with you if you want, but we have to get you out of here and to safety. There are commandos trying to kill everyone!"

"Oh, like they're going to believe you," Geren remarked, also in Arabic.

"Screw this," Kalid muttered, handing off his VEPR to Geren. "You can see I'm unarmed. Come on, we have to get out of here now!"

He started walking down the hall when a gunshot exploded at the other end. Geren lifted her VEPR, but Kalid stepped into the path of her muzzle, glaring at her for a moment.

It was a girl, crouched, with a pistol too large for her tiny hands aimed at Kalid. Between his boots was a section of floor where the bullet shattered tile.

"How do we know we can trust you?" the girl asked.

"Because you're aiming at my heart, and I'm putting my back in the path of a stream of autofire that can stop you from killing me. I'm not going to let my partner gun you down because you're scared," Kalid said. There was iron in his voice, and Geren let her finger ease off pressure on the trigger.

Above, gunfire was still shattering as desperate enemies fought against each other.

"Alex, the fighting's not slacking off!" Geren called out.

"There are kids here who don't want to leave their parents," the girl called out.

"What's your name?" Kalid asked.

The girl looked surprised. "F-Fayorah," she said, stuttering.

"Fayorah, we'll try and make sure everyone's parents get out, but…it might be too late for some of them," Kalid told her.

The crack of sadness in his voice made Geren's heart feel as if it were caught in a vise. Even though her brain told her that he was speaking about an organization whose goal was the smashing of her home country, her heart realized that he was speaking to the children.

"I know," Fayorah spoke up. "I can… I can…"

"Tell them to close their eyes, to protect them from the smoke," Kalid ordered. He looked back at the sprawl of corpses along the hallway. "Hold hands, and we'll walk single file out of here."

Fayorah bit her lower lip, looking back into her room.

She let the handgun lower to the floor. Over the gunfire, Geren couldn't hear her as her lips moved a mile a minute. Obviously she was coordinating the children with her.

Then, amazingly, a chain of children started out into the hall. Kalid took Fayorah's hand as she, too, kept her eyes clenched shut. He handed the children off, one at a time, to Geren, who began to lead them down the stairs and out into the lobby.

BOLAN NEARED THE TOP landing when he spotted a shape.

"Zimal?" a voice called.

Bolan quickly answered "Yes," hoping that the sound of the gunfight would make his accent intelligible.

There were more quick words in Arabic thrown down to

him as Bolan continued up. Dressed in his own combat blacksuit, he looked enough like the Egyptian commandos to fool them for the time being, especially under the stress of a massive firefight. As Bolan cleared the last of the steps, recognition dawned on the face of the commando, but it was too late.

Bolan reversed his M-16 and slammed the stock hard into the Uzi of the Egyptian. Slugs tore into the wall from the initial trigger pull, but the weapon was dislodged from numbed fingers. With a second flick of the M-16, the fiberglass stock crashed across the man's jaw, snapping him onto his back. Bolan moved forward and clamped his hand over the commando's mouth, giving one final club to the gunman's temple, making sure he was out cold.

Bolan felt the Egyptian's pulse, and found his skin to be cold and clammy. Shock was setting in on the guy and the soldier could see why. A pool of blood had spread where the man's leg rested on the tile floor as he was protecting the landing. Bolan pulled a roll of electrical tape from his battle harness and ripped the cargo pocket off the man's pants, wadding it up like gauze to form a pressure bandage. Taping the gunshot wound, Bolan at least stopped the man's bleeding, and proceeded to bind his wrists and ankles with nylon cable ties. He wouldn't go anywhere, and now the Executioner had a prisoner.

Interrogation would come later.

Bolan sensed a presence behind him and spun, bringing the M-16's muzzle down. He held off on the trigger when he recognized Alex Kalid.

"What are you doing here?" Bolan asked.

"Checking to see if there were any more kids up here," the adventurous ex-blacksuit said.

"I have a prisoner. Get him to our vehicle, and make sure that he gets back to the safehouse," Bolan ordered.

"But what about you?" Kalid asked.

"I'll hitchhike," Bolan explained. "This guy might have info we need."

"It's your shoe leather," Kalid proclaimed, yanking the unconscious Egyptian commando and hauling him over his shoulder.

Bolan gave Kalid a slap on the back and turned to look at the progress of the firefight.

There were two Egyptian commandos in the hallway, crouched behind walls, firing withering streams of lead at the Hezbollah defenders. To the right was an open window and a man at it.

Bolan slung his M-16 and pulled his Beretta. He didn't want to distract the commandos engaging the terrorists, and he wasn't intending to take them out of the fight. All confusion in this three-way fight was to his advantage.

The Executioner swung around and brought the front sight of the M-9 to bear on the Egyptian commando at the window. The guy was quick, reacting to Bolan's presence and raising his weapon halfway, but Bolan was just an instant faster, tapping out five sound-suppressed shots that punched the commando's ticket. He stood there, half dead, still struggling to bring up his weapon to avenge his own murder, then staggered backward and slipped out the window.

Bolan was already halfway to the window when he heard a cry of outrage from the ledge.

It was too late to turn back now, Bolan thought, hitting the window and levering out onto the ledge, barely a foot wide. He saw five Egyptian hitters crawling along the side of the building. The rearmost commando was bringing his Uzi around when Bolan fired at him with the Beretta.

Stone chips rained on the Executioner's head from the enemy's autofire. The gunner reacted as if he were lanced with a hot poker, but only pulled back tighter. Egyptians started disappearing through a window quickly, getting off the ledge. The injured commando fired off a ragged burst with his Uzi to try to keep the Executioner pinned down. Finally the gunner's fusillade ended when he was pulled in through the window.

The whole floor came alive with a suddenly increased rage of gunfire. The Egyptians had joined the conflict in earnest. Bolan stuffed his Beretta into its shoulder holster and gripped the depressions in the wall, creeping along the ledge as fast as he could.

His boot slipped, and his grip was tested against the ledge, his knuckles screaming in outrage at the sudden torture. Bolan fought to transfer his weight to the foot still firmly planted on the ledge, while he brought up his dangling foot, wrestling with gravity. Two fingers on his right hand popped loose from a depression. Bolan got his foot up, and with both legs under him, he redoubled his loosened grip.

It was only five floors, he thought. The fall would only shatter his spine and leave him needing tube feeding and artificial respiration for the rest of his life. Bolan shook the thought from his mind and continued moving sideways. He reached the edge of the window the Egyptians had entered and paused. He got out the Heckler & Koch .45, loaded and ready, Safety off. He transferred the gun to his left hand and turned on the ledge, his back to the wall.

The drop, in the darkness, looked farther than it really was. Bolan instead concentrated on his plan. He wrapped his right hand around the window frame, ignoring the bite of a piece of broken glass as it nicked his finger. The blood made his grip sticky and wet, each moment making it more difficult to use all the strength of his right arm to swing him around and to surprise the Egyptian commandos.

That moved up his timetable, forcing him to make the desperate swing before he bled too much to keep a good hold.

With a savage yank and a powerful leap, Bolan swung himself around, the big .45 blasting out rounds at the shadowy enemy warriors in the apartment.

8

Major Tofo didn't know who had followed them out onto the ledge, and he had hoped to cover his own back but the gunfire blasting through the door of the apartment was incredible. Already one of his commandos was lying facedown in a growing puddle of blood. Tofo's Uzi tore out buzz-saw bursts that ripped into the gunmen across the hall, shredding into them.

He glanced back at Janza who was holding his bullet-creased arm.

"Can you fight?" Tofo asked.

Before he could answer, a thunderclap drowned out all sound. It was one of the Soviet-made RGD-5 fragmentation grenades his men had carried with them. Like the Uzis, the grenades were deniable weapons. They also had the power to turn a small room into an abattoir of death and destruction. Its official casualty radius was fifteen to twenty meters, but more often, in the heat of combat, soldiers were too spread out to take more than nicks and minor injuries past all their protective gear. However, against a group of casually dressed terrorists holed up in an apartment, the blast zone was completely fatal. A wind of serrated steel passed through the doorway, but Tofo and his men ducked out of the jet of shrapnel propelled by the concussive power of nearly four ounces of high explosive.

Tofo checked his men. Three were alive, but Janza was

wounded. Hamid was dead, facedown, torn apart by rifle fire that had punched through him mercilessly.

Tofo went to the door and held out a small hand mirror to scan the hallway. He wasn't going to risk his head by poking it into an enemy line of fire. There were three more doors on this floor with desperate gunmen taking up defensive positions. One weapon opened up, and Tofo dropped the mirror, pulling his hand back in before it got shot off.

"They're still dug in," he said to his men. He pulled an RGD-5 from his harness and pulled its pin. He aimed for a spot on the far wall and swept his arm in an arc, releasing the grenade in a looping throw, then whirled back deeper into the apartment. The grenade bounced off the wall, skidding down the tile floor of the hallway.

Instants later, the building shook with the crash of the explosion. Screams filled the air and Tofo shouted. Janza was hot on his heels as the pair dashed across the hallway to the apartment they'd cleared out. Token fire chased them in the hall, but Dinal and Ramid, who were still hunkered by the stairway, cut loose with a merciless volley of autofire.

Janza had tied off his arm injury and was holding his weapon with both hands.

"Can you knock a hole in the wall?" Tofo asked.

"I have the use of both hands," Janza answered.

"Do it!" Tofo said.

Janza quickly went to the wall of one apartment and produced some det cord, fast-burning explosives inside a cord that was spooled out like thread. Using some putty, Janza made a concentric, man-sized circle on the wall and then stuck in a blasting cap. Tofo grabbed a table and held it up against the explosion. He and Janza used it as a shield.

Gunfire exploded through the window across the way, and Tofo looked there, seeing a man in black with a handgun diving into the apartment he was staging his assault from. The Egyptian major watched as a chest full of slugs cut down Amin.

Tofo tucked his chin to his chest, shoulders rising to protect the rest of his neck.

The det cord erupted on the other side of the table, giving only a slight push to Tofo and Janza. Tossing aside the furniture, the two of them dived through the hole they made, targeting enemy gunmen. The bastard in black would have to wait for later.

THERE WERE ONLY TWO Egyptian commandos in the apartment when Bolan came through the window, tracking. Only one turned, reacting in time to notice the Executioner deliver his death sentence. The SOCOM blasted a deadly line of holes through the commando's rib cage, tossing him lifelessly to the floor. The second Egyptian was spinning away from the wall, hands going to cover his ears. He saw Bolan but didn't seem that concerned by a tall, ice-eyed man tracking a handgun on him.

The detonation's shock wave slammed into Bolan like a giant's fist, and for the second time in a week, he felt his body seemingly unplug itself from his brain for a moment. His consciousness trailed his mortal frame as he was thrown against a sofa, knocking it over. Only the cushions on the sofa saved the Executioner from shattering his spine in his uncontrolled fall, and the soldier desperately rushed to get a sense of control back into his body.

His body folded up and he rolled, his toes touching the floor, knees straightening. His head whirled like a top inside, brain still on full rinse cycle from being put through the washer once more. Even so, he managed to get his gun lined up at the remaining Egyptian commando in the room, who had turned into a pair of gunmen. Bolan pulled his Beretta in one smooth motion, as the double-imaged killer went for his own gun, and fired at both of them.

Bolan's vision settled into a single image as he watched the double-dead gunman go sliding to the floor bonelessly.

The Executioner didn't have time to deal with his headache or congratulate himself on his shooting, as the hole blasted through to the other apartment suddenly became alive with Hezbollah killers. Pivoting, Bolan emptied both of his pistols into the improvised doorway between apartments, bullets cutting into the terrorists before they had a chance to trigger their weapons. At the same time, he dived for the cover of the sofa, even though the steel-cored slugs were already perforating the cushions. At least the sofa offered him concealment as he clung to the floor.

Autofire blazed as Bolan felt for the M-67 fragmentation grenade he had on his harness. Popping the pin, he waited for the slowdown in rifle fire. It came on cue—the Hezbollah terrorists, firing in unison, ran out of ammo in unison. Bolan popped up and launched the grenade right through the hole, the little fourteen ounce hell bomb caroming off the skull of one gunman as he fumbled for a spare magazine. Bolan ducked and rolled to one side. There were scattered cries of panic next door as the grenade erupted.

Silence reigned on the other side, and Bolan got to his knees. His pistols were empty, and he took a quick moment to reload them, stuffing them back in their respective holsters. He unslung the rifle from his back and dumped its partially spent clip, exchanging it for a fresh one. If there was someone left alive in the next room, he didn't want to get caught flat-footed.

Besides, the reloading gave his brain more time to recover from being slammed around. Even so, he popped some acetaminophen tablets down his throat. They'd stave off the effects of a compounded concussion for a little while more.

Bolan did an orbit of the hole blasted in the wall, looking through to sweep the entire room, giving himself as much cover as possible. He slowly divided the room into angles, giving his enemy minimal exposure. Nobody was moving. He stepped through the hole and felt a hand grab at his ankle. Bolan stepped back, sweeping the M-16 down, looking into the half-torn face of a Hezbollah terrorist. Gleaming skull poked through flesh, one eye cored out by shrapnel, his mouth gaping wide open, and a wail escaping from his throat as he awakened from the shock that reduced him to something out of a monster movie.

Bolan kicked free and fired a mercy burst into the gruesome features, hypervelocity slugs exploding the face and making it an even more nauseating mess.

He looked around. The door was open, but he wasn't going to risk taking fire from the other apartment. The gunfight had died down. That meant either the terrorists were dead, and Bolan was too late to get to Faswad, or that both sides were licking their wounds. He knew that the Egyptian commandos intended to leapfrog through the holes the drywall between the apartments generated with det cord. He stepped back and found the dead commando who made the hole he walked through. Sure enough, he had a spool of the stuff, and detonators.

Bolan quickly began unwrapping the cord off its spool and winding it around his fist. Then he stuck in a timer fuse. Taking it in the palm of his hand he walked back to the first apartment, then broke the cap on the fuse and tossed it out the door toward the stairway entrance. Spinning back, he dived through the gap to the next apartment, hitting the floor as the explosion ripped down the hallway. He kept his mouth open all the way, equalizing pressure between the inside of his head and the incredible crush zone outside his skull. By the time he somersaulted to his feet, swinging the M-16 up on its sling, he felt no worse than he had before the blast.

It wasn't saying much, but he bet the rest of the building certainly felt that kick. The plastic explosives were unfocused, and didn't have the shrapnel producing casing that made a grenade so deadly. However, with plenty of explosive punch, the ball of det cord did create a distraction.

Curses filled the air, followed by shouted orders. Bolan took a peek out the door with a pocket mirror and saw Faswad was sending out a wave of gunners to sweep the hallways. The Executioner slid a grenade off his harness, an AN-M8 HC smoker this time, but they wouldn't know about its purpose. They'd just see a grenade. This time it wouldn't produce a fatal shock wave, but a heavily concentrated cloud of white smoke. The smoke would be slightly toxic, but nothing fatal, and it would add just the right mix of confusion to allow the Executioner to get to Faswad.

He lobbed the soup-can-style grenade down the hall at Faswad, and saw the look of horror on the shell-shocked face of the terrorist before ducking back, assault rifles ripping the air where he was moments before. Men screamed and a window broke as a body down the hall dived through it. Bolan hadn't intended to take out another Hezbollah fighter, but one less gun was one less enemy shooting at him.

He heard the familiar sound of the smoke grenade popping and hissing as it vomited choking white smoke. With a swift movement, the Executioner wrapped his nose and throat with a black balaclava, then grabbed his M-16, charging across the hall. His target was not the suddenly blinded Hezbollah fighters, but the two Egyptian commandos who remained. The rifle in his hand chattered before he even made it to their last position, bursts sweeping at chest level.

Uzi fire snapped back in kind, chewing a segment of wall, giving Bolan a hint of where his enemies were in the darkened apartment, and he leaped, pivoting in midair. He was aiming for cover behind a padded chair and found himself landing atop another of the dead Lebanese gunmen who were fighting to defend their headquarters. Bolan wondered how many of these men had their families holed up on the second floor, and how many children could have died because their parents chose to ally with the wrong conspirator. The Executioner had seen such bloodthirsty tactics too many times before.

And every time it happened, he fought tooth and nail to protect as many young lives as possible. A passing thought told him that he'd turned many children into orphans in countless other battles with murderers and thieves. Bolan fought his way over it and the lumpy body of a dead Hezbollah fighter, rattling off another burst from his M-16 into the darkness. Uzi fire crashed and rattled, homing in on the muzzle-flash of the noisy rifle in his hands, and Bolan quickly crawled behind the cover of an overturned dining-room table.

Slugs chewed and pounded at the other side of the rectangular tabletop, and Bolan gave the M-16 a quick reload, feeding it a fresh clip. His plan was to take one of these commandos prisoner. It wouldn't be easy, but in case the other commando proved incapable of supplying information due to blood loss and shock, he'd need someone healthier.

Screams to his left roused the Executioner from his battle planning, autofire raking wildly into the doorway as Hezbollah commandos charged, their eyes rimmed red from the irritating smoke. Bolan levered his rifle around and cut loose with the M-16, chopping mercilessly into the chests of the first three gunners, raking them with half of the 30-round magazine. At that range, the hypersonic bullets hit hard enough to literally make flesh detonate, and the gunmen tumbled lifelessly, their torsos turned into soup by the impacts of Bolan's fusillade. The Egyptian commandos across the room were also laying down fire, hammering at the doorway when to Bolan's right, glass crashed.

It seemed like a lot of people were crawling the walls this night, and Bolan scooped up a dead fighter's rifle and hurled it. The AK-47 caught one invading gunner in the chest and unbalanced him, knocking him back out the window, screaming until he hit the ground.

Another gunner swung in and dropped to the floor, raking the wall with the Egyptian commandos, only to be perforated by twin streams of autofire. More gunners came charging through the apartment's front door and Bolan laid down another blistering wave of ammo, making the terrorists dance.

Gunfire halted abruptly. Ringing silence replaced the shattering symphony of violence that had gone on before. Bolan was out from behind the table, and he was looking at the last of the Egyptians, who was looking down at his slain comrade.

Bolan lunged, bringing up the M-16 to use it as an impact weapon on the enemy. Instead, the commando brought up his Uzi, deflecting the fiberglass stock with the steel frame of his weapon, and then snapping the wire stock of his own weapon into the Executioner's chest. Bolan stumbled backward, robbed of breath by the sudden impact, but not of his fighting skills. The Egyptian lunged at him and tried to bash the steel wire stock of his weapon into Bolan's skull, but the soldier ducked under the swing and hammered the barrel of his M-16 into the man's gut.

The Egyptian commando slammed back into the wall, but brought up one boot to catch Bolan in the hip, the impact nearly knocking his feet out from under him. Bolan dropped the M-16 and latched both hands on to the commando's battle harness, yanking him down hard. Bolan was aiming for a head butt, but missed as the Egyptian squirmed out of his way. A fist pumped hard into the Executioner's armpit, making him lose the grip in his left hand. With a violent twist, the Egyptian swung Bolan to his right, but the Executioner hooked his leg around the fighter's and slammed him to the floor, face first.

Bolan crawled desperately, grabbing at the Egyptian's hair and watch cap, but his opponent twisted hard. Skin tore and hair came away in a bloody clump, along with the cap. The Egyptian screamed and kicked the Executioner hard in the jaw, dazing him.

Bolan drew his SOCOM from its hip holster. He opened fire, but the commando was too fast out the door, racing to freedom.

Getting to his feet, Bolan started for the door when his boot bumped the corpse of the man who had managed to get in through the window. The face on the floor was familiar.

Imal Faswad.

Too late, too slow.

Bolan grimaced and limped into the hallway, looking around for more survivors, smoke still billowing from the grenade. Except for corpses and blast craters, the hallway was empty.

That's when the Executioner heard a fit of violent coughing. He followed the sound to where the smoke was thickest, seeing the bald-headed lackey who Faswad had so viciously dismissed only minutes before.

Minutes. That's how long this whole mess took.

Bolan pressed the muzzle of his .45 into the face of the bald man, grabbing him by his shirt.

"You speak English?"

"Yes…especially with a pistol rammed up my nose," came the answer.

"How much do you know about Kazan and the tanks?" Bolan growled.

"Enough to make you not want to shoot my head off," the gasping Hezbollah agent wheezed.

"Then we're going on a little trip. Come on."

9

Cabez looked askance at the big, grim figure sitting in the passenger seat of the old Volvo. The barrel of a cocked handgun the length of his forearm was aimed right at his gut.

"Could you uncock that gun? There's a lot of potholes in this part of town," Cabez stated.

"Drive more carefully then," came the answer. Cabez didn't like the voice this guy had—it reminded him too much of the sound of a shovel grating in hard-packed sand, digging a grave.

Cabez swallowed hard and drove around a patch of seriously cracked, broken pavement. The eyes of the big man never wavered from him.

"You have a name I can call you by?" he asked.

"I've heard that some people call me al Askari."

Cabez gripped the wheel tighter, sweat soaking his face now. "Oh God."

Bolan remained silent.

Tears began to sting in Cabez's eyes. "You didn't have to kill everybody in the building. We didn't do anything to the Americans."

"I didn't kill everyone. The children are safe. And those men in black weren't mine," Bolan answered with a sudden absence of harshness. "Your boss made a bad decision, got mixed up with the wrong business partner."

"Yeah, and now he's dead," Cabez answered, laughter

bubbling nervously from his lips. "We not only have al Askari, but someone else out to kill us all."

"If you tell me who your boss was dealing with, I'll make sure that you won't be bothered by either of us again," the big, brooding shadow next to him said.

"Sure. You'll kill me right away."

"You'll live. You have children to fend for. Get them placed. Give up your war. Try a more peaceful way to deal with Israel."

"It was the Israelis who came after us," Cabez growled back.

"No, it wasn't. They're Egyptian."

"Egyptian?" Cabez was stunned.

"Turn left here," Bolan ordered, waving the massive pistol.

"I know that the tanks came from an Egyptian. Someone with real pull and rank, but I don't have a name," Cabez said as he followed Bolan's directions.

"That much died with Faswad, for now. I'll get my handle on him somewhere else. But what are you doing with the other six tanks?"

"You're asking me to sign my own death warrant," Cabez said.

"I can always find someone else to take care of your orphans," Bolan replied.

Cabez felt himself spin. Whirling vertigo plunked him down and he stopped the car.

"Kazan is going to use the M1s as the tip of a spear for an assault on Nahariyyah."

"Where are they staging this assault from?" Bolan asked.

"From a camp five miles east of Naqoura."

The silence in the car was deafening, and Cabez felt his bowels clenching in anticipation.

"Keep driving. We're going to where the kids are."

Cabez, hand trembling, started the car.

THE EXECUTIONER HAD GONE against impossible odds many times before, but not against a strike force of tanks ready to

punch into a city. A half dozen M1 tanks, backed up by the
Hezbollah's standard T-72s would give them a chance against
Israel's war machines—at least to cause as much murder and
mayhem as possible before being destroyed or forced back
beyond the border.

But in the meantime, especially if the Hezbollah force
managed to get in to street fighting, the loss of life would be
enormous.

Nitzana, times ten at the least.

And Israeli policy was to exchange blood for blood. Three
or four thousand dead Israelis would be answered by twice
that amount in the bombing of Lebanon, taking a terrible toll
on cities where the Hezbollah received its support. Maybe
this time, Bolan grimly mused, it would push the entire region into a bloodbath of retribution, with neighboring nations
acting in response to their murdered citizens.

Bolan gave Cabez the Toyota 4Runner, since it was the
only vehicle that had the capacity to comfortably ferry the
orphaned Lebanese children, and locked his icy gaze with the
terrorist.

"Remember your promise."

Cabez flinched. "I won't let these children live without
families, and I will not raise arms except to protect myself."

Bolan gave the roof of the 4Runner a double slap, and
Cabez drove off.

He glanced back to Kalid.

"Our prisoner is named Anwar. He lost a lot of blood, but
your field dressing, and a couple liters of saline solution
have stabilized him." Kalid started the briefing immediately.

"You got his name?"

"He's giving us the name, rank and serial number deal.
Rust is running that through those computerized contacts of
yours."

Bolan frowned. "Egypt is an allied nation."

"Only just barely, since the fun and games in Iraq. I seem to recall a lot of rioting, angry people assaulting the embassy in Cairo."

Bolan shook his head. "People are entitled to their opinion. What was done was what was done."

"We're going to nip this war in the bud, though, right?" Kalid asked, with an almost childlike exuberance designed to bring Bolan out of his brooding.

Bolan managed a smile and a nod. "That's what I'm here for. I'll get some rest. You talk some more with Anwar. I have a feeling he and his friends got steered wrong on this particular mission."

"We'll awaken you come the eve, mighty Horus. I'll prepare some tanna leaves to replenish thy godly might," Kalid joked.

"Make it some strong coffee and a sandwich, and I'll be happy."

Kalid crossed his arms over his chest and bowed. "Yes, sahib."

Bolan's mood lightened, the strength returning to him even as he made his way to his cot.

As BOLAN SLEPT, Kalid sat, keeping watch over him. Using one of the safehouse's laptops, the young American was surfing the Web for information about Horus, inspired by his association of the soldier with the warrior-god.

Kalid found a quote attributed to the ancient god and smiled. "Yeah, that's impressive."

Bolan gave a toss in the bed, and Kalid worried that he'd awakened the sleeping soldier. But it was merely the troubled sleep of a man with too many sorrows. He looked at the quote on the screen and began to read. He wanted to impart the words of the speech into his mind.

"'I am Horus, the great Falcon upon the ramparts of the

house of him of the hidden name. My flight has reached the horizon. I have passed by the gods of Nut. I have gone further than the gods of old. Even the most ancient bird could not equal my very first flight. I have removed my place beyond the powers of Set, the foe of my father Osiris. No other god could do what I have done. I have brought the ways of eternity to the twilight of the morning. I am unique in my flight. My wrath will be turned against the enemy of my father Osiris and I will put him beneath my feet in my name of *Red Cloak*.'"

"Impressive," came a whisper from the doorway. Kalid's heart leaped in surprise. He turned to see Tera Geren standing in the doorway, leaning against the frame, arms crossed.

She was just out of the shower, her hair disheveled, still wet and uncombed. The scent of soap on her drifted to his nostrils and a heady drunkenness threatened to overtake him.

"Hey," Kalid whispered. He shut off the computer and got up, walking closer to her. He didn't want to disturb Bolan's sleep anymore. "How's Anwar?"

"He's fine," she answered. "And you?"

Kalid realized his face was almost touching hers as they spoke quietly. He started to jerk back, heart hammering as her green eyes twinkled alluringly. "Shook up. I killed two innocent men."

"We both went through a lot," Geren answered. "Do we have to talk here, or do you think he can sleep by himself?"

Kalid looked over his shoulder at the sleeping Bolan. "I guess he can. He just came in looking like hell."

Geren nodded knowingly as they walked to the living room of the safehouse. "I know what you mean. When I first joined Say…" She paused and looked at him. "Sayeret Duvdevan. Who are you guys?"

"A mixed breed. I don't even know who I'm working for. I'm just on loan from the FBI."

"And Russel?" Geren asked.

Kalid shrugged. "I think he's CIA. Not sure."

Geren nodded.

"You're not going to ask about Colonel Stone?"

Geren glanced back to the bedroom where Bolan rested. "I don't think he works for anybody."

"He is the cat that walks by himself," Kalid told her.

"I thought he was a falcon."

"He is a god of many aspects," Kalid said, winking.

Geren chuckled.

"So you're Unit 217?" Kalid asked.

Geren nodded. "I think I'm still with them, if they haven't written me off completely."

Kalid couldn't stop from blurting his next words. "They'd be pretty foolish if they did let you go."

Geren's freckled cheeks reddened. "Thanks."

Kalid clamped down on dozens of questions he wanted to ask her, the foremost in his mind being if she had a man back in Israel. He sat with her, the silence filling the room like a thick fog, everything else blotting out. Moments dragged on until the house became alive, Anwar talking to Rust in one room, Bolan getting up and clomping around his bedroom.

"We'd better attend to our guest and the big guy," Kalid said.

Geren nodded, keeping quiet. "I'll go check on Brandon. You see how things are with Anwar."

Kalid looked at his watch. "We didn't say a word for an hour."

Geren smirked. "Let's chalk it up to admiring the view?"

Kalid shrugged. "Or simple diplomacy."

Geren took a deep breath, and Kalid searched for something to distract him from the swell of her chest. "We'll have to work on your diplomacy, Mr. Johnson," she said.

WHEN BOLAN OPENED HIS EYES, it was to the bright light of the sun. Judging from its height over the horizon, he figured he had been asleep for a couple of hours. A catnap, one of those dreamless bouts of unconsciousness where he shut down to conserve energy. It was a pattern he'd grown used to in a lifetime where he often lived hand-to-mouth and picked up shelter and warmth between bouts of mayhem and madness.

He got to his feet and tested his equilibrium. He wasn't dizzy, and no bright floaters crossed his vision. If the explosion the previous night aggravated his concussion, Bolan couldn't tell. He took slow steps around the room, working to stretch out his cramped muscles. His stitches were still holding in place, and except for a mild cough, he was pretty much over the accumulated smoke and dust he had inhaled the night before. Fires, smoke grenades and vaporized drywall, it was a wonder that he wasn't choking.

Bolan poured himself a glass of water from the carafe that Kalid had to have set there, then peeled off his dirty shirt and threw it in a corner.

"You look like a road map," a voice stated behind him. Bolan turned and saw Tera Geren, holding a plate with the sandwich he'd requested earlier.

"Helps me keep track of where I've been," Bolan answered, looking down at the scars crisscrossing his chest, back and arms. He didn't remember every white streak of skin, every hairline impression, every scratch, but he wasn't one for concentrating on the souvenirs of his career. He was only there to do his job, not cover himself in glory.

Geren set the plate next to the water jug. "Need anything else?"

"An update on what's happening with Anwar," Bolan said.

She nodded. "Anwar's confused as hell. He and his team are Unit 777."

Bolan glanced at her with surprise. "The Egyptian counterterrorism unit. No wonder."

"No wonder you look like you hit a brick wall and bounced."

"Actually, it was a sofa."

"Well, Anwar and his unit were hitting the Hezbollah because they launched an attack from Egyptian territory. He was under the assumption that this was a reprisal, but he was iffy about the lack of intel. It was made worse when he realized that there were noncombatant children in the building."

Bolan set the sandwich on the plate after a couple of bites, his appetite fled. The night before, he came into conflict with soldiers on the same side, and killed some of them. They were soldiers who had been misdirected and misguided into action, but he still felt the pangs of guilt. In the middle of the night, in the heat of battle, there was no way to tell what was going on.

More friendly dead attached themselves to Bolan's soul, but this time, they joined him because of his hand. The commandos thought they were destroying a threat to Egypt, instead of closing a back door.

Bolan tried pulling himself from the shock and confusion. "Who did he say was in charge of the mission?"

"Captain Pedal Tofo. This guy is top of the line. A super pro," Geren replied. "Bad news and a half."

"Anwar said that?"

"Anwar said that Tofo was a real top-secret type. He's not officially part of Unit 777, but he managed to arrange for Anwar's commander to assign a team to him. They were sheep-dipped. You know what sheep-dipped is, right?"

"Taking conventional special operations forces, stripping them of their military identity, and then sending them into action where the military wouldn't normally be able to go," Bolan said. "Made deniable and sometimes expendable."

Bolan looked up, confused for a moment.

Geren knelt before him. "You're human. We didn't know."

"I vowed never to harm a soldier on the same side, and last night I personally killed at least…" Bolan tried to think of the night before, but the fog of violence and mayhem was too much. He just remembered muzzle-flashes and bodies convulsing in agony.

"I killed too many men who were supposed to be fighting the good fight."

"We didn't know. They were cutting through enemy terrorists like a chain saw through butter, and they were going to cut off our only link," Geren reminded him.

"I should have known better," Bolan growled.

"There's no way you could have known. And with the efficiency they were killing with, they could have ripped you to pieces if you used anything less than your full combat abilities."

Bolan looked into her green eyes, jaw set firm.

"Someone on Egypt's side set everyone up. They didn't care who died. Look at Nitzana. How many Israelis and Palestinians died there? People who were trying to live in peace even with extremists on both sides calling for each other's blood. This animal doesn't respect life, any more than the Hezbollah tank drivers cared about their own people."

"The tanks."

Bolan checked his watch. "I have to take care of Kazan and his tank force. He's going to launch a spearhead from a Hezbollah militia stronghold with the remaining six tanks that Faswad bought."

"Where?"

"Nahariyyah."

"Faswad wasn't thinking small," Geren said.

"I'm thinking that it wasn't Faswad on his own. His tank dealer probably suggested the assault, especially since the Israelis are building up for more tension in the south along the Egyptian border."

"But Egypt and Israel are allies."

"Cold allies. There's hard-liners on each side that still remember the old days. A long history of enmity—just the kind of thing a warmonger would love to exploit."

"We could call in the Israeli air force…"

"And tell them what? We think an Egyptian general sold tanks to your worst enemies in order to spark a war between Egypt and Israel?"

"And then we'd really have people itching for a war," Geren said.

"I have to take out the tanks myself."

"And what about us?"

"I still need to pin down the mastermind behind all this. Between you and Alex…"

"And Anwar."

"Anwar. I need to speak to him."

"Do you think that's going to be healthy?"

"We'll find out either way," Bolan said, pulling on a fresh BDU shirt and leading the way out of the room.

ANWAR FESJAD FELT THE BIG SOLDIER entering before he arrived. It was like a pressure wave, and even recovering from blood loss and several traumas, he recognized the blazing cold eyes of the mysterious warrior who had taken him down the night before.

He paused.

"This is your leader?" Anwar asked the man who had introduced himself as Alex.

Kalid nodded.

"You can call me Colonel Stone," Bolan told him.

Anwar eyed Bolan. "The rest of my unit is dead."

"At least one, maybe up to three, made it out."

On a wobbly leg, Anwar got to his feet. "And why were you there interfering with us?"

"I was going after Faswad myself. I needed to know who sold him twelve Egyptian-issue M1 Abrams tanks."

Anwar, aching, met the tall man's gaze unflinchingly. "Did you learn who?"

"Faswad was cold on his back by the time I got to him. The only survivor didn't know who Faswad dealt with, but he knew about another incident about to go down."

"So you think someone in my government tried to cover all this up?"

"Some extremist. He might have a following, but not enough to reach the Hezbollah in Lebanon."

"That's why he had his spook Tofo grab up my team and lead them to their deaths," Anwar said.

"I didn't know who you were," Bolan said.

"And we didn't know who you were," Anwar replied.

Bolan nodded. "You're free to back out…or I'll give you a gun and you can take it out on me."

"You pulled the trigger on my friends, but you're not the one who murdered them. If it wasn't your bullets that killed them, then it could have been the Hezbollah's. Someone else murdered my partners and fellow soldiers, and they also left you feeling like a murderer. I'm not letting that bastard escape," Anwar explained. After a morning of debriefing and discussion with Kalid and Geren, he knew they bore no malice toward the Egyptian counterterrorist team he was on.

Bolan nodded again. "The real murderer isn't getting away. That's my promise to you."

Anwar extended his hand. "I believe you."

10

Alex Kalid didn't like separating from the big warrior to whom he'd pledged his loyalty.

"I want to know if you're completely mad, or just bonkers from getting blown up too many times?" Kalid asked.

"If one man isn't enough to take out a column of tanks, what makes you think two will be?" Bolan asked in response.

Kalid shrugged.

"Which is why I'm sending you ahead to Cairo. You and Anwar and Geren are going to have to get things ready for me down there. I can't be in two places at the same time. Someone has to stop Kazan and the tank strike. And someone has to start picking up the trail of this Major Tofo before he gets 'cleaned up' too."

Kalid wanted to throw up his hands, but a pair of icy blue eyes held him still.

"Major Tofo brought several soldiers into conflict with me and you! You killed two men yourself, remember? You're going to let Tofo get away with forcing us into a blind friendly fire incident?"

Kalid looked at his hands. He still hadn't been able to wash all the blood off.

"Are you going to stick around Lebanon waiting to figure out how to take out a division of unstoppable war machines?"

Kalid clenched his fists, then looked at Bolan. "Tofo's mine. I'm going to chew him up and spit him out."

Bolan looked him over, then nodded.

It took an hour for Kalid to realize how the savvy soldier had brought focus to his rage. Anger was at once a motivator, and a risk. Too much anger blinded a man to what had to be done, or pushed him to act as a total savage without regard to who he encountered. But too little anger in combat was also something that left one open to fear. He needed just the right cut, and Bolan, in his wisdom and skill, had honed that edge just right.

MAJOR TOFO AND WHOMEVER he was working for were in Egypt—that was where they needed to look for answers. If that meant leaving one man to impossible odds, then no matter how much it crushed the loyal heart of Alex Kalid, he'd do what the big man asked. The villains of this affair were not going to be allowed to escape to freedom.

Or, if the slaughter intended at Nahariyyah was only a feint, then Kalid was going to have to find a way to slow down what further madness they intended.

The more Kalid thought about it, as he explained to the others in the Peugeot, the more he felt that the Hezbollah assault was misdirection.

"You're right," Anwar said. "If they're supposed to be starting a battle between Egypt and Israel, why give the Hezbollah all the work unless it's to spread the Israeli Defense Forces thin."

"Double the incursions means double the defensive forces everywhere. We have enough to make the northern and southern borders a wall of steel. The same with the Golan Heights. Israel has all kinds of defensive barriers, and the forces with the skill to make any incursion impossible," Geren said.

"Unless there was something else," Kalid spoke up.

"Something that could open up a gap in a wall of Israeli armored divisions?"

"Anwar?" Kalid asked.

"Don't ask me. Except for the fact that Egypt now has tanks that can match Israel's, but if our mystery man gave as many as twelve away…" Anwar answered. "Maybe he has other technology."

"Like maybe aerial firepower?" Kalid asked.

"Something like that," Anwar stated. "But I can't think of any Egyptian pilots who would be willing to lead a bombing excursion into Israel. A handful of planes wouldn't provide the punch necessary, and this force would still be undermanned."

"Say that again," Geren said suddenly.

"What?"

"Still be undermanned?" she repeated. Kalid watched her green eyes flicker with activity.

"Unmanned craft. The United States had been using Predator Unmanned Aerial Vehicles to take out enemy antiaircraft sites and even moving vehicles with Maverick missiles," Kalid said. "You're brilliant."

Geren smiled. "You only say that because it's true."

"So our mystery man would have perhaps an entire squadron of unmanned aerial vehicles. With the right missile loads…" Anwar trailed off. "That could punch a very damaging hole through Israeli defenses. Or turn another couple of settlements and towns into charnel houses."

"He'd need a runway," Kalid said.

"That narrows it down…" Geren muttered.

"It's a start," Anwar spoke up.

"Let's not miss our flight," Kalid said.

A DIRECT ASSAULT WAS OUT of the question. Even the Executioner, laden with his usual kit of weaponry, couldn't hope to annihilate a division of tanks before they got rolling and under way in a naked display of firepower.

Bolan knew that tanks could be dealt with in an easier manner, but only if he was stealthy enough and fast enough. Speed and silence didn't always go hand in hand, but the soldier would have to make do with an uneasy balance.

Naqoura's lights painted the evening skies purple in the distance, the Hezbollah camp itself draped in camouflage netting that subdued the amber lamps illuminating its grounds. Guards were on patrol, and Bolan knew that this was more than just a simple Hezbollah operation by the presence of top of the line T-72B tanks—Syrian battle tanks, not the older 1960s and 1970s vintage. Even being a late 1980s model, the T-72B had the ability to launch guided missiles from its 125 mm smoothbore cannon. Only its relatively thin skin and the need to stop to fire its guided weaponry made it vulnerable.

The M1A1s could fire on the move and direct-guided fire easily.

As a combined force, the M1s pulverizing a path and laying down cover fire for the stationary T-72s, they would be a fearsome force.

They might not get to Nahariyyah unimpeded, but Bolan knew that actually destroying a city was just the icing on the cake. The armored fist smashing in through Israel's northern border would send the country on red alert. They were already hyper reactive over the blitz in Nitzana.

If the Hezbollah and Syrian forces were assumed to be taking offensive action from the north, it would start a whole new conflagration of destruction.

Bolan checked his war load. In addition to his usual combat kit, he had with him a drag bag loaded with high explosives, culled from several sources during the day thanks to J. R. Rust and Anwar Fesjad. A raid on a hidden cache of arms stored by the Egyptian special forces in Lebanon gave the Executioner a little extra edge against the tanks, even if it meant that he'd be slowed down.

With a sweep of his binoculars, he confirmed what Cabez had told him. Six M1 tanks and twice as many T-72s, an armada of armor ready to pound into Nahariyyah, sat waiting. Eighteen tanks, which could brush even a soldier as experienced as the Executioner aside like an insect, were ready to be stung.

Bolan slipped down into the darkness, hauling the drag bag into the deepening shadows of evening, cutting closer and closer to the compound. Reaching the fence, he found himself by the latrine runoff and garbage fill. The stench was incredible, but Bolan had smelled worse. Using a pair of rubberized, conventional wire cutters, he snipped through the chain-link fence. It was slower going than with the can of liquid nitrogen from the night before.

It was only twenty-four hours since he'd met Tera Geren, but the Executioner dismissed the compression of time. He was aching and stiff, but each flexing of his muscles, hauling on the bag, was one more step toward loosening himself up. When he'd opened enough of the fence to crawl through, he pushed his drag bag in first, then followed, bending the chain link back into position so it wouldn't betray his entry. A cable tie helped to secure the fence link in place.

Bolan quietly opened the bag, pulling out the first of several SLAM munitions. The Selectable Lightweight Attack Munition was a one kilogram explosive mine small enough to fit into the pocket of a BDU, yet with the capacity to punch through 40 mm of rolled homogenous armor at twenty-five feet. He wasn't under the delusion that the minibombs would destroy the tanks, but they would certainly leave the Abrams as fifty-ton paperweights and the T-72s in shambles. For maximum effect, the Executioner figured one fitted to each tread of each tank, and one under the main gun. Robbed of firepower and of mobility, the armored vehicles would be left useless.

That was the plan.

Whether Bolan could get the charges placed was an unknown. Over fifty pounds of high explosives were going to be slowing him down in addition to his gear. The soldier paused and checked the weapons from the Egyptian armory. The SLAMs were items shared with Unit 777 from the U.S. Special Forces who cross trained with them. So was the Heckler & Koch MP-5 SD-3, one of the quietest autoweapons ever made. On full-auto, with high-velocity ammo, it sounded no louder than a flock of pigeons suddenly taking to flight. Bolan was also pleased to note that the weapons cache had a .44 Magnum Israeli-made Desert Eagle to balance things out.

Bolan was off, sliding through the shadows, loaded for tank and terrorist. This was going to be a fast and dirty hit and git. Place the SLAMs, kill anyone who tried to stop him before they raised an alarm, and tear his way to an escape while nearly twenty armored vehicles got punched through with explosions.

Bolan did his best not to be seen, keeping low and crawling, the unblinking eye of his HK scanning the darkness. He didn't have night-vision goggles, but even in the darkness, he had more than enough light to see by from distant light sources. His own eyes were sharp and acutely capable of picking up movement in all but pitch-black conditions.

The rows of tanks were covered with canopies of camouflage netting, and in order to keep the tanks from being noticeable, their engines were off, and no lights were on. Guards patrolled in the darkness, and Bolan recognized that the operation was very high priority. Instead of the usual battered old AK-47s, the soldiers were armed with FAMAS rifles with mounted flashlights and the guards had the black sheaths of ballistic nylon vests.

The Hezbollah and the Syrians were really pulling out all the stops. Bolan figured that the Syrians were using the Palestinian group as an intermediary in their constant cold war with Israel. The well-armed and well-equipped mercenaries patrolling the parade grounds removed the last bit of doubt that the armored fist was going to be deadly and effective. The joint forces were using professional soldiers, and no doubt there were professional tankers who would use their vehicles with every bit of precision and skill that the Israelis possessed.

Bolan crouched by a tent, watching the guard movement, getting their timing down, then looked to see if there was a way to bypass them. They moved precisely, and their gaze was everywhere. They weren't going to make it easy for him to slip past, and they weren't going to drift to laziness and relaxation, as he'd experienced so many times before.

Professionals, however, were just as vulnerable as amateurs, and just as deadly. Bolan could anticipate a professional's actions. No amateur's diversions were going to turn these men aside. And the instant one was out of sight of the other, there would be milliseconds to take the guard, if even the sound of a silenced weapon didn't alert the gunner immediately.

No, the Executioner couldn't count on his usual run-and-gun tactics, the audacious violence of action that could freeze an untrained man into paralysis. He'd have to be better than that to hope to have a chance to get to the tanks and cause them damage before fighting his way back past them. Bolan surveyed the layout, then lifted the hem of the tent he was next to, peering inside with his hand mirror.

The tent was packed with fuel drums.

It was a shame that the drums weren't closer, Bolan

thought for a moment. Again, Kazan and his forces were proving professional enough to keep fuel and ammo and other supplies spread far enough apart. He didn't even think this was all the fuel for the tanks, and the other tents, spread twenty feet apart, would be able to protect their contents should one detonate.

Bolan's eyes narrowed.

A detonation would attract attention, but it would put the guard on alert.

A fire, on the other hand…

Bolan sliced a vent in the tent and slipped inside. It reeked of fuel fumes, and the lack of breathable oxygen forced him back out of the tent. Every ounce of his strength went to keeping from gasping for breath, coughing, and attracting attention. Finally he got his lungs back in working order, breathing slowly and evenly, his brain no longer fogged by the heavy weight of diesel in the air.

The Executioner felt in his usual combat harness and found a thermite packet with a remote detonator. With thermite to cut through the side of a fuel drum hull, and then to ignite it, the Executioner had his means of diversion.

It was a thin chance at diversion. He'd have to get some distance between himself and the tent for his ploy to work, and even then, there was no guarantee that more guards wouldn't be dispatched to protect the parked tanks. However, the separation of the tents and the vehicles did give Bolan the hope that the camp would only respond to the obvious disaster and its potential to damage the other fuel and ammo supplies, rather than be concerned about the fire spreading across the lane to reach the tanks.

By touch, Bolan set the thermite against a fifty-five-gallon drum of diesel, setting the radio command detonator. He withdrew from the line of storage tents and crab walked along, the MP-5 tracking for sentries who might cast their glance his way. Each moment Bolan delayed was another chance he could be spotted. If he failed, there was always J. R. Rust ready to phone in the necessity for an Israeli air strike to smash this camp to bits, and blow any chance of finding the renegade Egyptian pushing Israel to the brink of war, and perhaps sparking the bloodshed he sought to prevent.

Bolan being dead would only be an incidental detriment to failing, but he had long ago accepted the fact that one day he'd end up stopping a bullet, or being too close to ground zero of an explosion.

Whatever his fate, the Executioner would meet it without flinching, and most likely still trying to accomplish his mission.

It was do or die time.

MOHAMMED KAZAN HADN'T heard from Faswad or Cabez since the day before, and he was getting anxious. The plan was to make the strike at the crack of dawn the following day. Consulting his watch, he realized that to make the deadline, he'd have to start fueling and stocking up the tanks so they could get on the road by three. However, he didn't want to cause too much activity right now. He had a narrow window ahead when he knew American spy satellites and spy planes wouldn't be watching this part of the Lebanese coast.

It wasn't common knowledge that America kept a close eye on the border between Lebanon and Israel, but with Syria's occupation of the nation, it was only logical. Kazan had amateur astronomers watching the skies for him, as well as more sophisticated means from his commanders back in Damascus. Faswad was missing, and his headquarters hit, but Cabez had managed to call in. Not that the Syrian really wanted or needed the blessing of the Hezbollah. It just made things easier for him to operate against their common enemy.

Coordination.

Even if the Hezbollah was only good for being a line of bodies to stop Israeli bullets.

Kazan checked his watch. The regular patrols were still overhead. It was a Briton, he'd heard, who was giving out the overflight information about the spy satellites. Whoever it was, he gave good information, and his sky watchers made double certain. The West, with its vaunted high technology, was ignorant and helpless.

Something flickered outside his window, and Kazan immediately felt his stomach knot. He turned back and saw that flames were leaping from one of the tents.

He threw open the window, regardless of any possibility of a sniper in the area. "Get that fire under control!"

His men were already in action, reacting to the billowing column of smoke flashed with fire.

Kazan looked to the skies instinctively, knowing that while he couldn't see the satellites above, they could probably see the fire in that tent. Someone could not have vented the tents recently enough, and something set off the fumes, causing a fire that built to a flash point. There were any number of ways that the fire could have started in the tent; he'd seen these fires start before, almost spontaneously.

His paranoia was currently screaming otherwise. He scanned the hills around the complex, bringing up his night-vision binoculars.

Nothing moved. He lowered the glasses, spun and picked up the phone, wondering if maybe attack helicopters were hiding below the horizon, waiting for a chance to lock their Hellfire missiles on any tank that powered up.

They'd be too low, though, for any allied radar sources to detect.

Kazan looked out the window. His men were reacting to the fire like a well-oiled machine, and even the guards on the scene were keeping up their patrols, despite spending spare moments glancing at the flickering insanity of the tent fire. Soldiers with shovels tossed mounds of sand onto the fire while chemical fire extinguishers pumped out clouds of ice-cold carbon dioxide. It was no good, but luckily diesel fuel lacked the explosive properties of gasoline.

He stepped back from the window and reached for the mouthpiece of a communications uplink. "What's the condition of our perimeter patrols?"

Kazan frowned. He brought up his night-vision binoculars again and scanned the camp. The flare of the fire made them almost useless, and the bulk of the camouflage netting over his parked tanks made any further attempts at scanning useless.

But still, there was that prickling on the back of his neck. Danger was near.

BOLAN HAD FINISHED with the fourth of the M1s, taking advantage of the chaos of the fire to do his work, and started toward the fifth of the tanks. He'd developed a quick pattern, placing the SLAM mines directly on the axle, angled inward. Taking out the treads would be a delay of days. However, punching right through and into the drive train would take far longer to repair. Even popping one of the wheels that worked the treads, in addition to shattering the only means of propulsion for the tank would involve repairs that the locals didn't have the parts or skilled labor for.

Then there was the SLAM mounted just under the barrel, aiming inward. Bolan was intimately aware of the location of the M1's magazine from blueprints from the trip to Lebanon. He slipped the munition under the turret. With the boxy hull of the tank acting as a backdrop, the SLAM would slice its blast up and into the turret's relatively weak underside. If the tanks had any ammunition on board, the resulting jet of explosive force would be magnified by 120 mm shells detonating.

Bolan paused, detecting movement behind him. Voices were calling, and the camouflage netting billowed as someone swept it aside opposite the first row of M1s.

He hadn't even had a chance to mine all of the M1s, and they were sending in guards to double-check on the tanks. In the darkness, they might not spot the munitions that Bolan hid behind wheels or under turrets, but there was still the risk they might. The soldier hit the dirt and crawled under the fifth tank, holding a SLAM in one hand and the radio detonator in the other.

At least he'd wreak havoc on the armored force by setting off the charges he had planted.

Flashlights pierced the shadows, sweeping along the massive tanks as they sat like dinosaurs, sleeping through the din and ruckus of desperate men putting out a fire. One spill of light splashed under the tank Bolan was nestled beneath, making him squint as it reflected off a metal tread. He looked and watched the cones of illumination continue on either side of the tank he was under.

He'd hidden his charges well, stuffed deep into cracks his hand could fit into, and not much else. Luckily the SLAMs were no larger than his hand, despite the weight of their explosive charge and command detonation antenna.

Bolan eased out from under the tank, looking around as he heard a cry that sounded similar to "all clear" in Arabic. He didn't trust it and kept crouched, senses alert for the sound of boots through dirt. There could have been other sentries crawling among the tanks, without flashlights.

So far, he noticed none, but Bolan kept his MP-5 ready as he reached under the turrets of numbers 5 and 6, placing his magazine-blasting charges.

The Doomsday numbers were tumbling, and they were all sliding down to land on his neck.

He weighed the possibility of moving out from under the camouflage netting to the tent for the T-72s, but realized spending a long time among the T-72s, especially now since they were being checked over, however cursory the inspection, would be stepping into view of his enemies.

Instead, Bolan reached in and spent a few moments activating the antennas on the remainder of his SLAMs in his war bag, leaving them there, stuffed behind the shadow of the sixth tank's treads.

He slipped out from under the camouflage netting after looking both ways. He primed a high-explosive grenade from off his vest and judged the distance to the chain-link fence. It was a mere forty feet, so Bolan crouched low, in case any shrapnel came back his way, then aimed on an angle until he had a spot of fence seventy-five feet or so away, and out of line of the sentries who'd passed the tanks.

The spoon pinged as the grenade flew from Bolan's hand and he dropped low into the dirt.

The ground shook, the air hissing with flying bits of steel.

In his own explosion of motion, feet pounding, Bolan crossed the distance to the hole he made big enough to drive a pickup truck through. Long strides ate the yards in a matter of moments as gunmen scrambled to see what the hell was going on. A few opened fire to rake the hill above the perimeter fence, not realizing it was someone breaking out, not breaking in. As soon as Bolan reached the dust cloud that obscured the hole he'd blasted, he paused and knelt. The radio detonator came to his hand, and Bolan hit the thumb stud.

One gunman began tracking a line of AK fire toward him when the shock wave erupted from the six M1s.

The night turned to day as the fireball licked into the sky, the shock wave tossing enemy soldiers like rag dolls.

Bolan smiled as, for the first time in the past few days, he witnessed a massive detonation that didn't send him knocking around the countryside like a soccer ball.

11

Mohammed Kazan, heading out of his barracks, was halfway to the parked M1 tanks when they went up in a staggering flash. Unprepared for the detonation, he staggered backward, tripping into a Syrian guard racing after him. The collision between the two of them was a head knocker, and Kazan was slammed to his knees.

Even before he saw stars from his head bouncing off another man's, he registered muzzle-flashes in the distance, swiftly following a small explosion. At first Kazan thought the blast had come from one of the barrels in the fuel tent, but his mind swiftly narrowed in on the sound of the blast originating toward the fence, on the far side of his tanks. His men started firing, and then suddenly...

Kazan cleared his head.

"We've got an intruder!" he bellowed.

Men were still torn. Those who were fighting the fuel fire were literally floored by the sudden shock wave. One man had been tossed into the blaze and came running out, screaming, covered in the flower of flame, arms flapping like some fiery phoenix. Others were picking themselves up, their FAMAS rifles raking through a thick cloud of billowing smoke, trying to track a target that was on the other side of the immolating tanks.

"We've got an intruder! Get him!" Kazan shouted, hauling a Beretta from his hip holster and charging forward. He cut around the back, vaguely aware of his men. He saw the camp's fence and a single shadow disappearing over the top of the ridge.

Kazan opened fire, his Beretta cracking, spitting brass and flame. His fellow gunmen cut loose too, but he knew it was already too late.

He turned to look at the ruptured tanks that were vomiting flames. This single man had found the weakness of his mightiest weapons and torn them apart. He didn't understand why the whole camp hadn't been pounded into oblivion by a sudden assault of strike fighters, but he knew that if the mysterious saboteur was allowed to go free, the camp and its Syrian specialists were compromised.

"We need to get to the trucks, now!" he barked to his men.

BOLAN FELT THE BULLETS slicing the air over his head, an entire swarm of high-velocity slugs parting the air with their miniature sonic booms. His boots skidded in the sand as he cut down the other side. His wheels, a Volkswagen Beetle, lay waiting across a hundred-yard dash over scrub and sand. Long legs pumped, digging in on the loosely packed ground, making each step take more effort than it should, but Bolan clutched the MP-5 tightly, knowing that if he slipped and stumbled he'd lose precious moments.

He was under no illusion that the camp wasn't awake and ready to tear across the roads of Lebanon to hunt him down, even if they were in a section of the nation that Syria didn't "allegedly" control. Hezbollah was known to allow the Syrian army to enter their area of control to shell civilian areas in Israel itself. After fifteen seconds, Bolan was at the VW, and he skidded to a halt, body slamming against the curved little car.

He tore open the door and slipped in, tossing the submachine gun onto the seat next to him and firing up the engine.

Sand flew as the rear wheels spun, then caught and the Volkswagen gave a momentary fishtail, pulling out onto the asphalt, revving along.

The little car wasn't the kind of high performance machine that the Executioner would have chosen, but it was as tough as a three-dollar steak, and it was reliable, all the things that Bolan appreciated in any piece of equipment he used. He glided the compact vehicle down the road, keeping the speed relatively low so that he wouldn't attract attention. He glanced out the window and scanned his back trail.

Headlights.

A line of headlights.

Bolan pumped the gas and worked the transmission into Fourth Gear, pushing the little Volkswagen as fast as it could go. The road began whizzing by outside and he tore along. The speedometer, set for metric measurements, told him 120 km/h. A bit over seventy miles an hour, he figured. He worked the wheel, watching the rearview mirror as much as the speed of his vehicle would allow. Dust began exploding off the asphalt behind him in a series of straight lines, the telltale puffs of bullets impacting on the ground, chewing it up. The steering wheel dragged against his knees, and steering was an exercise in banging his elbow against one door and his shoulders against the car seats. Bolan wished he had something with more legroom, but the Beetle was practically invisible in Lebanon.

The Volkswagen was tough and reliable, but against small-arms fire it wasn't going to be much good. Bolan was getting pressed hard, and he coaxed more speed out of the engine. Bullets pinged off the back of the VW and he winced, realizing that the rear-engined automobile was vulnerable. He spun out and hit the parking brake, doing a 180-degree turn. Bolan shifted back up into Fourth and plunged toward the pursuing trucks, Peugeot pickups by the look of them.

Gunmen were trying to adjust for Bolan's sudden swerve and change in tactics. A couple of bursts of autofire slammed into the windshield, and the slender window frame turned into a twisted mass of broken glass. Bolan swept up his MP-5 and pounded its stock through the shattered glass. He swerved between the first two Peugeots and saw there were more behind them, two pickups and a pair of two-and-a-half-ton trucks that had their canopies pulled away, the men inside poking their rifles out hoping to be in on the kill.

Bolan fired off short bursts, first into the oncoming pickups, then sweeping one of the big trucks with the rest of his magazine. He avoided one out-of-control enemy Peugeot by swerving out of the bigger truck's path.

Bolan looked for the rearview mirror, but realized that it was gone with the rest of the front windshield. Instead, he checked the side mirror and sure enough the two lead pickups were in hot pursuit. He glanced away just as he heard the smash and crash of metal plowing through metal.

One pickup suddenly crumpled into a mass of mangled flesh and metal under the front grille and wheels of the heavy troop truck.

Bolan hit the parking brake once more, and the Beetle spun.

Escape wasn't possible, not with the relatively low speed of the old Volkswagen, but right then, running wasn't paramount on the mind of the Executioner. He'd been suckered the night before, and these punks who were set to launch an assault on helpless human beings were just the right people to feel his own fist of rage.

MOHAMMED KAZAN FLINCHED as he watched the other Peugeot suddenly crumple like a cheap cup under the wheels of the troop truck, the screams of the dying filling the air. His face reddened with rage as he watched eight good men mangled, and the troop truck stall as it got the remains of the smaller truck caught in its front axle.

Kazan cursed, scanning the road for the Volkswagen that had darted along behind the troop carrier. "Kill him!"

"The truck is bouncing, we can't get enough of an aim!" one of his men explained.

Kazan, in a fit of fury, rammed his elbow into his impudent subordinate's face, blood flying from a shattered nose and teeth. He winced as he pulled an incisor out of his skin, then looked around. "Where is he?"

"There!" another gunman called out. He brought up his FAMAS and held down the trigger, its muzzle-flashes ripping the night as the little Beetle came around the truck, aiming right at the hurtling Peugeot. Behind the Beetle, other trucks were trying to catch up to the scene of the mayhem, having overshot in the confusion.

Suddenly a massive boom sounded from within the Volkswagen, and the rifleman laying down the blistering fusillade jerked. A fist-sized hole punched out of the back of his skull, and the soldier flopped lifelessly at Kazan's feet in the pickup's bed, his rifle clattering out of the truck. The Syrians struggled as one of their own gave his final thrashing in the back of the vehicle.

"Sweet prophet," Kazan breathed as the mystery cannon continued to roar. His arm suddenly went numb, and he looked over, seeing that the joint had been shorn away, only threads of muscle and sinew holding his arm to his body.

Mohammed Kazan screamed as blood geysered from his gory wound.

BOLAN RETURNED his Desert Eagle to its holster as he gunned the Beetle past the Peugeot, its engine snarling. The pickup swerved to one side, and he kept his foot on the accelerator, bracing the MP-5 across his thighs to feed it a fresh magazine of Parabellum rounds, then tossed it on the seat next to him.

More fire came sizzling after him, but the two pickups were too far back.

Bolan hit the brake, then worked the transmission into Reverse. The Beetle swerved back in between the trucks that jerked to avoid getting wrecked. Bolan hit the brake again, sweeping up his MP-5 and holding down the trigger. Bullets pumped off into the bed of the first Peugeot, and riflemen in the back screamed and shuddered. Perforated corpses went tumbling lifelessly into and out of the back of the swerving vehicle.

The other pickup was swinging around trying to catch up to him, and Bolan tromped the gas again, steering with one hand while his free hand groped in the back seat for a replacement for the emptied submachine gun.

Fenders glanced off each other, and Bolan had to grab the wheel again with both hands to keep from flipping over. He looked back over his shoulder and spotted three trucks, two seriously depleted of gunmen, hot on his trail. One troop truck was chugging along after picking up the Syrian mercenaries from the big transport jammed atop the other pickup.

"Bring it," he whispered as he gunned the VW and sent it vaulting off the road, moving so fast it leaped the roadside ditch and landed twenty feet beyond, in dirt and scrub. Officially gone off-road, he had an opportunity to slow down and lean back, pulling up a SPAS-12 shotgun loaded with antiterrorist grenades.

The Executioner brought up the shotgun and triggered the first round at the leading pickup. The grenade shot like a rocket into the windshield of the truck and the cab suddenly detonated, ball bearings hurtling out in a cloud of flesh-slashing devastation that would have killed people in a ten-

foot diameter on open ground. Inside the cab, though, it reduced the driver and the gunman in the shotgun seat to pulp.
Driverless and out of control, the truck went sailing into the
ditch, grille crumpling and men tumbling out of the back,
bodies flying and bouncing off the earth. Several of the gunners' bodies were bent and smashed at impossible angles.
The other two Peugeots tried to leap the ditch, but Bolan ignored them for the moment, taking aim at the troop truck racing up behind them, emptying five more rounds out of the
grenade-spitting shotgun.

Bolan ducked as bullets came slamming into the hood and
doors of the VW, and he gunned the engine again, steering
away from the road without exposing his head to the streams
of incoming autofire. He reached into his holster again and
pulled the Desert Eagle and Beretta, letting the shotgun drop
to the seat beside him.

Kicking the door open, he hit a crouch using the entirety
of the little car as a shield. Engines roared as the pickups orbited the VW in a hard drive, looking for Bolan in the shadows. Rifle fire stitched the ground trying to seek him out, but
Bolan cut loose with both handguns, pumping 9 mm Parabellum rounds and Magnum manglers at the truckful of
angry fighters trying to tag him. The Peugeot peeled away,
trying to accelerate and Bolan swung around the back of the
VW as a second truck came shooting toward him.

Bolan fed the Desert Eagle a fresh mag as it had locked
empty. The Peugeot slashed past, again fenders scraping and
crunching against each other. The rush of wind of the passing truck ripped the breath from Bolan's lungs and he swiveled, the .44 Magnum pistol in his hands as he acted like a
turret. Eight slamming .44 Magnum shells tore into the truck
toward its rear wheel well, and the Peugeot suddenly jerked.
The rear wheel tore off its axle, and the driver struggled to

keep control of the speeding vehicle. Instead, the pickup did a flip, bouncing and smashing onto its top. Anyone inside was dead or trapped, so Bolan popped his empty magazine, slamming home a fresh stick of eight heavy caliber slugs, sliding around to the passenger side, and then doing a belly dive down the curved hood of the VW as FAMAS rifle slugs rained down on the stuck little vehicle.

Shoulder crashing into the dirt, he felt bullets pumping into the ground around him where the shadow of the Beetle didn't protect him from autofire. Curled up, Bolan swiveled on one hip. More slugs tore at him and the Peugeot screeched to a halt right next to the rear of the shot-up VW. Bolan popped up and pegged a Syrian gunner with his Beretta, spraying his brains out with a 9 mm mangler. In his other hand, the Executioner unleashed the thunder of his Desert Eagle, putting four slamming missiles into the windshield where he figured the driver and shotgun rider would be.

Returning his focus to his Beretta, he swung the front sight onto another FAMAS-toting gunman, punching a pair of hot 9 mm slugs into his gut and knocking him backward. The killer struggled to bring his black, bugle-shaped rifle up again, and Bolan adjusted his aim, punching a slug into the rifleman's groin. The shooter folded up, and Bolan swept his Desert Eagle along the bed of the stalled pickup.

Gunfire crackled from the road, slugs tearing again into the shell of the Beetle, and Bolan charged, taking cover behind the Peugeot. No line of slugs chased him yet.

Breathless, Bolan reached up into the truck bed and felt his forearm grabbed by an iron claw.

A blood-spattered face leaned over the truck bed, teeth bared in agony. Bolan tried to tear his arm free, keeping his free hand ready to fend off his enemy's strike. Pulling back hard, the Syrian in the truck bed suddenly showed why he wasn't using his other hand to pound on the Executioner. His shoulder had a chunk the size of a grapefruit blown out of it.

"You bastard!" Mohammed Kazan spit.

Bolan dropped his hand to his knife, drawing it in a single fluid motion. The blade swung up and creased under the jaw of the one-armed Syrian, but the blade bounced off the hard, stringy cartilage of the terror master's windpipe. Swinging the blade's handle, so the heavy knife was in an ice-pick grip, the Executioner jammed the point between Kazan's neck and shoulder.

The grip loosened some, but wild eyes still promised that Kazan wouldn't let go until he and Bolan both were riddled with bullets.

The Syrian didn't count on twelve inches of razor-sharp steel jammed between his head and his body. With a brutal wrenching motion, the Executioner finished off Kazan.

Bolan let the knife drop and he lunged in, grabbing a .223-caliber FAMAS rifle and a couple bandoliers of ammo that had been thrown into the bed in haste.

Diving over the tailgate, Bolan aimed the rifle with one hand, the T-shaped bullpup design allowing him to use the rifle with one hand easily. The muzzle lit up his section of the desert, and tracer rounds in the magazine showed the autofire walking across the front of the troop truck, tearing through the windshield. Bodies were still pouring out of the truck, return fire flashing at him.

Bolan hit the ground behind the wheelbase of the truck and fired under the frame of the vehicle. Bullets were now chasing him, and the soldier saw several pairs of legs. Feeding in a fresh magazine, he targeted them. A long burst and Bolan slashed through the legs of the Syrian murderers with a scythe of .223-caliber Remington death. Bodies dropped to the ground and the air was laden with banshee wails of agony in addition to the staccato rattle of autofire.

Bolan rolled along the back of the truck, dragging the bandoliers of FAMAS ammo with him, reaching the front of the Peugeot just as a hail of withering fire made the back of the truck lurch. The tires were blown to shreds, and the axle broke under the hammer storm. Bolan caught sight of the gunners focusing on the rear of the truck and swept them with a figure eight of his own. Three gunmen slammed into the ground as two more dived for cover. Hot slugs impacted the dirt near Bolan's face, making him duck back farther behind cover.

At least three more shooters were on the other side of the pickup, and Bolan was pressed hard. He'd been in this position before, and he wasn't about to panic.

He drew back from the Peugeot, putting ten yards between himself and the truck to get a better view of what was going on. Four gunners were advancing slowly. They were concentrating on the truck, and not beyond it. Bolan unleathered the Beretta, ramming home a fresh magazine. He was going to get as many of them off guard as he could, and the sound-suppressed pistol, though at the extreme of its range, was the only tool for this bloody trade.

Front sight obscuring the torso of one gunman, Bolan had his first target and he opened up with some quick shots, two to the chest and one to the head. The rifleman twisted and fell over, his partner spinning, looking in shock at the dead man. Before he could open his mouth to cry out, Bolan popped a pair of rounds into the other rifleman's head, brains exploding into crimson mist that drifted in the glow of headlights. The other two gunmen opened fire, raking the night in a wild panic.

Huddled to the ground, Bolan waited out the panic storm of autofire, then drew the Desert Eagle and slammed a single round through the armored vest of one of the last remaining gunmen.

The last rifleman, his weapon empty, screamed in horror, beating on his inactive weapon as he tried to get it to work again.

Bolan instead rose to his feet, walking slowly toward the man. Tears were streaming down the rifleman's face as he fought to somehow get his weapon to work.

"Stay away!" he cried in English, hands waving at the tall man in black, slipping toward him like a razor blade descending on a wrist.

"You speak English?"

The man finally dropped his rifle, crossing his arms before his face.

"Do you speak English?" Bolan repeated, grabbing a fistful of the Syrian soldier's armored vest.

"Yes! Yes, dammit, I speak English," the Syrian sobbed.

"I have a message for Damascus," Bolan growled. "Al Askari didn't approve of Kazan's operation."

"Al…al Askari… The Soldier?" the Syrian asked, his throat clenching on each word.

"Yes."

"Please!" the Syrian screeched. "Please…do not send me to hell."

Bolan yanked the smaller man nose to nose with him.

"I want you to tell your masters in Damascus that I will visit them soon. Tell them to kiss their families goodbye as soon as they can, for their blood will flow in an unstoppable torrent. Do you remember my message?"

The squirming soldier repeated it.

"Run! Go back to the base and pray I never see you again!"

Silence descended on the battleground as the remaining gunman fled.

This mission wasn't finished, but the Executioner was back on the road to seeing justice served.

He wouldn't feel fully redeemed until he finally destroyed the mystery devil and his tools.

12

The flights from Beirut to Cairo were uneventful, because all three members of Bolan's advance team had the wisdom to go completely unarmed.

Alex Kalid didn't like the feeling of nakedness when he traveled unarmed. He was on the job, and there were people out there ready to kill him and his friends. Sure, he could probably handle a single threat, but he couldn't protect the others if they were ambushed with automatic weapons.

This weighed on him as he got off the plane. They had all traveled separately, arriving in Cairo International Airport on different flights. It was a safety precaution, so they wouldn't be seen as a single unit. Meeting later would entail checking into a four-star hotel only 10 miles from the center of the city.

Kalid decided to get to the hotel before the others and scout it out, before entering and checking in last. This way he had some control over the situation. Forewarned was forearmed, the cliché went.

Clichés, however, have enough truth to them to make them worth paying some heed.

Cairo, being on one of the largest rivers in the world, had plenty of trees and beautiful greenery for a tourist to sit among. Kalid placed himself on a park bench, stretching out to enjoy the sun that hadn't risen far enough yet to make the city cook. He paid attention to the Egyptian soldiers who were sitting at the entrance to the hotel. Their presence didn't set off Kalid's danger sense. Egypt stationed soldiers at all of its hotels, as a means of protecting tourists, or at least tourist revenue.

With pitchers of hotel-supplied ice water, and a plate of snacks, the soldiers sat and chatted, keeping their eyes on the people coming and going. They were lions at the watering hole, Kalid thought. They watched to make sure that the water hole wasn't disrupted, even by their own kind.

Pulling out a paperback novel, he pretended to read, all the while his eyes scanning beyond the pages of pulp action and lurid sex.

Tera Geren showed up, dressed in a checkered blouse, a baggy denim jacket and jeans. The doorman took her backpack and nodded. She slipped him a tip, then scanned the area.

Her eyes met Kalid's for a moment, and he tried to fight down the stirrings under his belt.

She was a beautiful woman, cute and cherubic especially given her height, if you hadn't seen her in action. Even with that, there was a sense of innocence about her. She wasn't a brutal killing machine, and Kalid did his best to dismiss his association between her and recent Israeli policies in the occupation of Palestinian buffers.

He didn't blame the country or its people. Still, fifty years of resentment smoldered in the ashes of the Arab world's defeats.

Even Egypt, whose leader Anwar Sadat had given his all toward achieving peace with Israel, had elements still within its government, and without, who desired nothing but a cleansing bloodletting that would push the hated Jews into the sea. Kalid knew that Muslim extremists were a problem. The fact that they now had someone operating with some of the power of the Egyptian military behind him was bowel-tighteningly terrifying.

That fear was only pushed aside by the gut-churning rage that he was suckered into gunning down fellow terrorist fighters. The same kind of men who would have fought to shut down the operation if they knew exactly what it was about.

Sudden realization hit.

Tera Geren.

He felt a strange sickly realization that he was somehow linked to her. Kalid knew that such things happened, and his queasy fear was that he might compromise the mission because of a stupid action. Even worse, he thought of the sudden, brutal possibility that Geren would be torn from his life. He didn't like it. He'd only just met her, and yet he had bonded with her. They didn't agree politically, but there was a deep, abiding trust between them.

Kalid watched as Anwar Fesjad finally showed up. There were enemies out there, and by the fact that the enemy was hidden, yet in authority, they were unknown. A simple police officer, given Kalid's description as a potential terrorist, would be in his full rights to pull his gun and burn Kalid to the ground.

Would he have the will to shoot an honest lawman or soldier?

Curses burned deep within his heart of hearts as he got up, collected his bag and prepared to check in.

The only way Kalid would find out what he would do was to step into the future and do it.

TERA GEREN OPENED the door to her room and threw her backpack in the corner. She kept her mouth shut, looking around. It was no secret that most hotel rooms held surveillance devices, especially in the capital cities of each nation. She'd even discovered, on a trip to Washington, D.C., a fiber-optic camera in the showerhead of her bathroom.

Needless to say, she was glad she was posing as a French-woman and spent a lot of her time over the bathroom sink, not exposing herself to whoever was snooping on her. Just because the United States and Israel were allies didn't mean that an agent of the Mossad was going to willingly show her naked body to an American Peeping Tom.

Geren leaned against the sink and looked at herself in the mirror. Under her eyes were dark circles from too little sleep and too much stress. She felt as if she were a hundred years old and she'd been slapped for every year she was alive. Closing her eyes, she mentally flashed on the image of Alex, his smiling face, his skin the color of creamed coffee spread across tight, firm muscles. Outside, when she saw him watching the hotel, she felt something hit her in her belly, an emotional firecracker that spiraled around inside her when their eyes met.

This wasn't some cheap paperback or spy movie.

This was real work.

People were dying, and she had a bullet wound along her rib cage to prove it.

But Alex…

She had to admit to getting into discussions with him just to talk to him, to hear his warm soft blend of accents playing in her ears. While Colonel Stone was spending his time sleeping and recovering from sudden violence, they'd had a chance to talk and become familiar.

A familiarity that swept aside their initial contempt.

There was a knock at the door, and she went to it, seeing Kalid's smiling face.

"Oh, sorry, wrong room," he said, then slipped in through the door.

Geren shook her head to indicate that she hadn't had a chance to scan for bugs or cameras.

Kalid pulled out a field meter from his bag and held it up. He nodded to her. They were being snooped upon.

Geren hated that his deep, dark eyes drew her in so easily. She was supposed to be a professional, on a top-secret mission, with no time for such shenanigans.

"Alex...I don't know," she began.

"Nobody will ever find out," he answered her, role-playing, then brushed her hair out of her eyes. Her skin tingled with electricity.

She bit her lower lip, wavering. "Don't do that."

Kalid recoiled from her, surprised by her statement.

"I'm sorry..." he said.

"You don't know how crazy that makes me feel," she whispered. Kalid gawked for a moment, and she put her hand on his chest, leaning close so he had to stoop to hear her barely breathed words. "I know we set up like we were having an affair..."

She let her phrase trail off and her lips brushed his neck below his ear. His hands gripped her arms tightly, and she wondered if he was going to throw her off him. Instead, his grip relaxed and his own breath was brushing down her neck.

"Are we acting?" he asked.

Geren looked up at him, stunned. "I'm not."

She was surprised at her own admission, as if she suddenly started speaking in ancient Sumerian or Martian. The words were cut off from her own brain, and she shrunk away for a moment.

Kalid's eyes softened and he let her go. "Neither am I... but I'm not pushing myself on you."

She bit her lower lip again. "Okay."

She took his hand, backing up and leading him farther into the room. Her heart hammered, the room was swimming, but her grasp on his hand was the only thing keeping her anchored in reality right then. She could see his arousal and looked out the window. She wanted to close the shades, but she didn't dare let go. If she did now, she'd never recover her will to go through with whatever charade they had set up. They'd have to get to work instead of continuing on with this madness.

Kalid orbited her, still keeping his hand in hers, and drew the curtains shut, lowering the room into darkness.

"Are you really attracted to me?" Kalid asked.

"Uh-huh." She stretched up and kissed him full on the lips for the first time, tasting him. There was a moment when his whole frame stiffened, trying to resist giving in to hormones, and then he pressed harder against her, meeting her kiss with his own, tongue slipping to entwine with hers.

The pair found the bed in the darkness and worked together until they had drained every ounce of fear and anxiety.

ALEX KALID COULDN'T believe himself as he lay naked against Tera Geren's curled figure. They were here to work, to be seeking out an Egyptian conspirator, not soaking the bed sheets with their sweat and other bodily fluids. He reached out, stroking her hair, and then ran his hand down her arm, feeling her smooth, flawless skin.

She shifted and buried her face in his bare chest, her fingers reaching around his back and tugging him tighter. He could stay that way all day, and taking a quick glance at the glowing red numbers of the clock, he realized that they had been together for five hours. He'd drifted off an hour ago and was just coming back around again. The crimson glare of the LED numbers stared at him like the angry eyes of a demon.

He was shirking his duty, betraying his loyalty.

Geren sensed the shift in him. "You're awake already?" she asked.

Kalid nodded, a futile gesture in the darkness. So he gave a grunt of an affirmative.

"Is it time to go to work?" she continued to inquire.

"Just about," he whispered.

"Oh," she answered. She rolled off the bed and was moving to pick up her clothes quickly.

"Tera…"

"I understand," she answered. "There's still daylight left. We could get some leads tracked down."

Kalid was out of bed, suddenly feeling very self-conscious, even though he was barely visible in the shadows. Geren clicked on the bathroom light and was bathed, harsh white light splaying off her skin, making her look like porcelain. He stepped back as she hugged her clothes to her chest.

"I wasn't kicking you out of bed…"

"No. I was. I felt stupid for hopping into bed with you like a silly schoolgirl."

Kalid nutted up the courage to step forward and wrap his arms around her, her jeans and jacket wadded between them, as if acting like a barrier to further arousal.

"I'm supposed to be a professional. And not a professional who spends most of her work in bed, dammit."

"That wasn't work. That was something we both needed."

Kalid shook his head. "God, I don't know how the hell to say this."

Geren rose on her tiptoes and kissed him. "We'll figure it out," she said. "Okay?"

Kalid nodded and slowly broke the embrace.

Geren closed the bathroom door, giving herself a modicum of privacy as Kalid turned, scratching the back of his neck. He flicked on the lamp and began looking for his clothes when he looked at himself in the mirror over the dresser.

All he could see was an accusing face, wondering why the hell he tortured a good woman's feelings by giving in to his carnal desires. She was a co-worker, she was a partner and she was someone he might care about.

Kalid lowered his head, breaking eye contact with the inquisitor in the mirror, pulling on his boxers and then his cargo pants. Working alongside "Colonel Brandon Stone" or "Striker" or whoever he really was was a dangerous job, and Kalid knew it.

Both he and Rust were showing signs of their recent near-death incident in Beirut. Kalid's ears still rang intermittently from such close proximity to a stun grenade going off in the room he was in. Kalid put on his khaki bush shirt. His biceps were tight against the sleeves and made him feel physically strong, even if the disappointed glare of his own reflected eyes told him that inside, he didn't have the strength to take another step.

"Where's my shoes?" he asked himself, breaking away from the mirror once more as he heard a knock at the door.

Kalid slipped into his loafers, forgetting about his socks. He checked the peephole and saw Anwar's face filling the fish-eye view.

"Been wondering where we were?" Kalid asked, opening the door.

There were three men standing there. Anwar's shirt was drenched with blood.

"I'm sorry, Alex," the Egyptian croaked.

GEREN FINISHED cleaning her face. Being jarred back to reality was unsettling, but somehow she managed to get her feet back underneath her.

She understood the urgency to get back to work. Alex probably felt like a naughty child, sneaking off to play doctor when they were told to do their homework. A bit of resentment filled her at the thought of the world demanding their attention when she had entered a wonderful fantasy only moments before. Geren finally stuffed that feeling back into its Pandora's box, wrestling it shut.

This was not a job for hopeless romantics. Even if she couldn't be a cold-blooded killing machine like Stone, she still had to keep her wayward thoughts in line. A moment's inattention could spell death for herself or her partners.

There was a knock that resounded even in the closed bathroom. She wondered if that was Anwar, then heard Alex's voice outside. She went to open the bathroom door. Anwar's voice croaked unhealthily on the other side of the thin balsa wood door.

Hearing Alex curse, Geren stepped to the clothing rack, quietly slipping the travel iron off its mounting. Whoever was on the other side of the door was watching Alex like a hawk. They probably knew he was a full-blown physical threat, even if he was unarmed. Geren didn't doubt that.

"Where is she?" a voice shouted.

"Man, are you her husband or something?"

Alex was still trying to keep up appearances, even if they had Anwar.

There was a meaty impact. Alex had to have been hit. She winced at the thought of his being hurt, sympathetic pain stinging her as she clenched her only weapon tighter.

"Check the bathroom," the voice ordered. Geren's stomach turned. So much for hiding out. She knew sooner or later she'd have to act.

The doorknob turned and Geren slid behind the door, not wanting to give her opponent too much opportunity. The door opened inward, a pistol-filled hand leading the way.

Geren swung down with the iron, using the weight of her weapon to multiply the wrist-crushing force of the attack. The pistol suddenly flew from numbed fingers and a cry of pain started from the lips of the gunman. That cry was instantly cut off as Geren swung upward, bringing the iron hard into the hollow of the man's jaw. The point of the travel-iron's boat shape plunged into soft flesh and the man staggered backward, gagging. He collapsed, hitting a lamp and smashing it to pieces.

Kalid and Anwar both moved as one, lunging at the other gunman. Geren caught a glimpse of Kalid, his shirt smeared with blood from a cut on his cheek, then turned and scooped up the intruder's pistol. It was a single action Helwan pistol, and she checked to make sure the safety was off.

The gun was on Safe, hammer at full-stand, and she realized why. These guys didn't want to attract the attention of the soldiers at the front of the hotel with any gunplay. Geren swung into the hotel room and saw Anwar peeling the gun out of the grip of the other intruder as Kalid hammered mercilessly on his head.

"We've got guns," she said, holding her aim on the man she had ambushed with the iron. He was holding his throat, looking none too healthy. She kept her distance, not wanting to get into a wrestling match. Sure the gun was on Safe, but if it got out of her control, this guy knew how to use the gun and get off at least one shot.

Gunfire would attract unwanted attention.

"On the ground, facedown, hands laced behind your head," Geren ordered.

"If you shoot…" the Egyptian said.

"I'll ram the muzzle of this right into your belly. All the noise and all the muzzle-flash will go right into your soft flesh, creating a destroyed area the size of a honeydew melon," Geren growled.

The Egyptian saw her face and knew she wasn't bluffing. All Geren knew was that there was a freight-train-sized rush of blood roaring past her ears, making things almost impossible to make out. She was succumbing to tunnel vision, and she had to break that.

Geren noticed the door to the hallway was open, and she closed it quickly, pressing her back to the hard wood.

"Alex?"

"This guy isn't going anywhere," he answered. He stuffed the other Helwan into his waistband, then looked over at Anwar.

"I'll live," Anwar said.

"Where's the blood coming from?"

"It came from a couple of slices on my chest, but mostly they kept punching me in the face and a lot poured down from my nose and mouth," Anwar answered. "They cleaned off my face to stick in front of your peephole."

"They knew where we checked in?" Kalid asked.

"They were waiting for me in my room and jumped me like Geren jumped that one fool," Anwar answered.

"How screwed are we?" Geren asked.

Anwar peeled off his bloody shirt, wincing. "These won't be the only guys."

Geren realized that her bloodied companions were going to need clothes.

"Strip!" she ordered her prisoner.

"And if I don't?" the intruder asked.

Kalid grabbed the belt of the other intruder and held it between his hands like a garrote. "I'll pop your fucking head off. You won't be able to scream. And you'll die quietly."

Geren was amazed at the dark rage simmering on lips that minutes ago had lovingly caressed her.

The Egyptian began rapidly pulling out of his shirt.

"Got your tape?" Kalid asked.

Geren nodded.

"We'll cover up Anwar's cuts," Kalid told her. "Go get it. I've got this creep."

Geren had turned to her backpack when she heard a strangled gargle. She froze but didn't look back, even when she heard the sound of heels thumping and digging into the carpet. Pulling out a roll of white medical tape and a small box of gauze, she finally turned.

Kalid was garroting their attacker anyway with the appropriated belt. The man's face was purple. A savage twist was accompanied by the sound of nuts cracking, and the digging heels stopped moving.

Geren waved Kalid and Anwar into the bathroom. "I'll watch the door. Clean your wounds first before anything else happens."

Kalid paused, looking at her, dark soulful eyes searching hers.

He was looking for forgiveness for the stone killer he'd turned into.

Geren pulled her gun, but cupped his untorn cheek. "Clean your cut, all right?"

He nodded and kissed her forehead.

"Hurry up. These guys aren't going to be alone."

13

The Executioner was on a quick flight out of Lebanon to Cairo. It was before noon when he got on the plane. He'd had plenty of time to wash off the stench of blood and smoke from his body, slipping into jeans, combat boots and a black knit shirt. Using a Peugeot that wasn't particularly splattered with gore and with a minimum of bullet holes, he'd sped back to the safehouse, abandoning the tough little Volkswagen, its engine and tires savaged beyond all possible use.

Rust had used his embassy ties to get them onto the flight. Inside a diplomatic pouch were Bolan's Desert Eagle, Beretta, knife and spare magazines.

Instinct told Bolan that the world didn't revolve around his actions, and as he catnapped in the jet, flashes of injured and killed allies across the years popped through his mind. He tried to fight his dreams, but only ended up popping his eyes open, mouth dry, and a tinge of sweat just under his hairline.

"Are we there yet?" Bolan murmured.

"You kids ask that question one more time, and I'm turning this car right around," Rust answered.

Bolan managed a tired smile, reaching for a bottle of water. "You missed your calling as a stand-up comedian."

"The Improv's loss is Langley's gain," Rust answered. "You doing okay?"

"I'll live," Bolan said. "What's our ETA?"

"Another fifteen minutes and we'll be at Cairo International. Depending on how paranoid our enemy is, we'll have an hour of fooling around with customs over our diplomatic pouch while our embassy in Egypt is consulted," Rust explained.

"Two hours to catch up with Alex and company."

"More or less," Rust replied. "Why?"

"My gut tells me our friend is going to be expecting us." Rust grumbled.

"I want you to head to our alternate."

"Sure, the one-star hotel off the tourist map?" Rust asked. "And while I'm endangering my life in squalid conditions…"

"I'll be endangering my life looking up our advance party."

"You think it'll be that serious?" Rust asked.

Bolan stared out the window. "I've never had things go one hundred percent smoothly before. It's too late to start now."

TERA GEREN STEPPED into the lobby, her heart a trip-hammer. Tucked under her loose denim jacket was the flat frame of the 9 mm Helwan pistol, her backpack slung over her shoulder, dangling like a purse. If the Egyptian soldiers out front were going to stop her, she promised herself to be cold and calm.

Getting caught with an unlicensed firearm would only be the start of her troubles.

No, Geren thought. The start of her troubles was when she was assigned to keep an eye on Faswad and figure out what he was shipping from his farm-machinery plant. Things just went tits up from there and never recovered.

Geren walked past the table of Egyptian soldiers, getting a couple catcalls from a few of the more bored and lascivious men. She didn't mind and considered adding an extra shimmy to her walk, shaking her butt before realizing that it was half covered by her jacket. She looked down at her waistband. The jacket had shifted and panic filled her mind as she wondered if any of the soldiers had noticed the gun.

No shouts of rage or commands to stop greeted her ears, so her panic subsided.

Her butt had been a perfect distraction.

She gave thanks for sexism and continued strolling down the road before stopping and leaning against a wall, breathing deeply.

A figure walked with purpose up the road. It was Anwar. She gave her lower lip a short chewing. She wished it was Alex. It was a silly thing, but the longer he was out of her sight, the more she worried about him.

What if he was stopped? What if the backup team for their kidnappers got him?

"Are you okay?" Anwar inquired, stopping beside her.

"Ask me in a day or two," Geren answered. "What's keeping Alex?"

"He's just hanging back, giving space between our leaving," Anwar told her. "We're on schedule."

"Time flies when you're having fun," Geren said, not sounding entirely convinced.

Anwar smiled, and Geren's tension cracked some.

"Let's move down a couple more buildings. There's a fruit stand there, and we can act like shoppers," Anwar suggested.

"Good idea," Geren said, looking back over her shoulder.

Kalid stepped out onto the sidewalk and kept moving, not betraying the fact that he saw Geren and Anwar ahead of him. He was in full professional mode, and that meant he sensed something coming. Something wicked and deadly.

The gun in Geren's waistband suddenly felt heavier. They didn't have the firepower for any kind of violent engagement. Soldiers along the hotel row wouldn't care who was on whose side, either. The easiest targets always got hit first when a firefight came around. On foot, and unarmored, without much in the way of cover, Geren defined herself as an easy target.

"Anwar," she said, still watching Kalid catching up.

Something popped to her side. It was a sickening pop, wet and thick, and it took Geren a moment to realize exactly what that sound was. With sickening dread she turned to Anwar, who was holding his stomach.

Anwar looked at her and said, "Run."

Geren froze for a moment, then saw Anwar's hand drop from his stomach, blood burbling outward. A silenced rifle bullet, the analytical part of her mind deduced. Quick. Deadly. Efficient.

It felt like a freight train rammed into Geren, and she thought she'd been shot. Gravity released as she went sailing over the branches of a roadside shrub, then she hit the ground, feeling two hundred extra pounds of weight draping on top of her. She struggled, trying to pull free from the grappling arm smothering her, when her vision focused on Kalid's face.

"Snipers!"

Geren went for her gun, but Kalid grabbed her wrist.

"If we start shooting, we'll be the only ones with noisy weapons," he hissed. He glanced up, and Geren followed his gaze. The bush wasn't much protection against a bullet, but it was concealment, at least for now. "The Egyptians aren't going to be looking for a sniper with a sound-suppressed rifle."

"Did you see them?" Geren asked.

"No. I just poured on the speed and tackled you."

"How pinned down could we be?" Geren asked.

"I'm not taking that chance, but no follow-up shots came at you. You were an easy target," Kalid told her.

"I was just telling myself the same thing," she said. "Anwar…"

"He died quick."

"He had time to tell me to run."

"Damned good advice," Kalid whispered. "Come on!"

The pair rushed off down the side street, keeping to the cover of tree trunks.

BOLAN SWUNG THE RENTED Audi TT onto the street where the hotel was located. He had an explanation for his feeling of dread as he spotted soldiers, their rifles out, surrounding a body facedown in the street. Bolan clenched his fingers white-knuckle tight around the steering wheel as he caught a glimpse of the man lying lifeless on the ground.

The familiar features of Anwar Fesjad stared at him, but the open eyes would never see anything again.

"Move for the ambulance," a soldier said through the open window of the Audi.

Bolan was jarred from looking at the dead man's eyes.

"I'm sorry… I've never seen a…" he began, choking. A master of role camouflage, his ability to appear innocuous had helped him often in the past.

"It is all right," the Egyptian told him.

"When…when did it happen?" Bolan asked, continuing to play the role of the innocent tourist.

"Don't worry. This was the only man they shot. We think the killer ran off when we came running."

"Did you see anything?" Bolan pressed, looking around.

The Egyptian patted Bolan on the shoulder. "You are safe under the protection of the Egyptian army, friend."

Bolan grunted an affirmation, looking in the surrounding crowd for a sign of Kalid and Geren. Nothing. He thanked the soldier and drove off, taking care not to give in to his impulse to tear around the corner and try for their alternate hotel.

There was no guarantee that the others were heading in that direction. Bolan made a couple of turns and headed down to the park, which was on the way to the dive where he'd sent Rust.

At the same time, he tore open the diplomatic pouch with his free hand, drawing the Beretta, just in case.

KALID KEPT CHECKING over his shoulder as they continued along the winding path through the park. Palm trees abounded, as did benches for tourists to sit at as they looked upon scale duplicates of some of Egypt's amazing wonders. Kalid, from his previous time in the country, knew that the duplicates were there so that tourists wouldn't have to wade through the garbage-strewed originals, or ride in pickup truck convoys across lung-choking sandy dunes.

Besides, Cairo wanted to keep money in the city, not out in the wild expanses of wilderness where tribesmen were willing to sell or cut throats for their living.

"Think we lost them?" Geren asked.

"I'm not even sure how many we were supposed to be losing," Kalid answered.

He was running on fumes right now, disoriented by the fact that one of their own had been blown away. He knew why no subsequent bullets had chased them down, and it wasn't because he was faster than a speeding bullet.

Anwar was a security risk, so a bullet was put through him to make sure he couldn't help them anymore.

Kalid and Geren, however, were to be kept alive, perhaps even herded along into another trap. The mystery mastermind had to know what they learned.

Kalid scanned the path ahead, knowing it was too late to turn back. He gripped Geren's hand tightly, fear clutching his gut like the ice-cold claw of a dead zombie.

Geren seemed to react to his fears, drawing realizations of her own. She gave Kalid's hand a squeeze and nodded in the direction of the road parallel to the serpentine path they strode.

Kalid spotted them. Four burly men, some of the biggest

men he had ever seen, were approaching. Kalid was not a small man himself, but he was only one man.

He swept his gaze over the area, looking for a way out, and saw two more coming from the other side. He tensed and looked at Geren. The noose was being drawn in tight.

"When I say so, start running, fast," Kalid whispered.

"I'm not leaving you behind," Geren answered.

"Don't be stupid. I'll be kept alive if they catch me. But they don't need two prisoners."

Geren scanned the scene. "We can shoot our way out."

"Sixteen, maybe eighteen shots between us? Maybe. But what if they have gunners as backup?"

"Alex…"

"Go!" Kalid ordered.

He whipped the Helwan from his waistband, shoving Geren away. She paused for a moment, and Kalid fired his first round between her feet, the sand kicking all over her sneakers. The woman finally broke and ran, charging between two hulking forms who were trying to sandwich her. Kalid opened fire, his stream of Parabellum rounds intended to make noise and send people scrambling. The Egyptian thugs shied away from the gunfire, giving the tiny form of Tera Geren a chance to slip between them at full speed.

For someone with short legs, she ran pretty fast.

Then his Helwan locked empty and Kalid tossed his gun aside, swinging and bringing his elbow up and into the face of an Egyptian muscleman reaching his long brawny arms out to grab him. The man's face exploded in a splatter of blood from a broken nose, head shocking backward. Kalid lunged at him, riding him between two other thugs. He delivered a hard-edged karate chop to each of them, striking them in the ribs. It didn't knock them out as if in a cheap martial-arts movie, but it knocked the wind from their lungs and gave Kalid some breathing room. He had managed five long strides when a body slammed into him, arms groping around him. Kalid reached down and sank his fingers into the Egyptian's crotch, closing his iron grip and twisting.

A howl pierced his eardrum, making his head hurt even more, but the big man grabbing at him let go enough for Kalid to ram the heel of his palm under the exposed jaw. He staggered. Another hand reached for him, fingers clawing and tearing at his shirt.

Kalid planted one foot solidly on the ground and brought the other up, smashing the upper chest of his latest assailant, knocking him down. The man clutched his breastbone, his face showing agony.

Kalid tried to get farther. He swiveled his hips to avoid another tackle and continued his plunge, hoping to draw the crowd of big men with him.

The ground erupted in a gout of sand, a shock wave slamming into his face.

Kalid tried to muddle through it, but he was off balance and stunned. Some part of his brain told him it was a stunshock grenade, but most of his mind was of the general consensus that unconsciousness was a preferred condition.

Hands grabbed at Kalid's arms, but he still kept twisting and fighting, trying to cut free. His knee impacted with a stomach, and his toes collided with someone else's genitals, but it was too little too late.

The fists began descending on Kalid's head and chest.

Blackness swiftly descended.

GEREN PAUSED AS SHE heard the crash of an explosion in the park. She was filled with dread. That dread took human form when she spotted a pair of the hulking thugs sent after them. Without regard for the Egyptian hotel guards, she pulled her Helwan and fired into the chest of the man on the left. He jerked, clutching his rib cage.

The other man didn't even pause, instead picking up speed to catch up to Geren.

She shifted her aim, but then dived to the ground as the angry hardman went sailing over her head. With a twist, she was on her feet again, bringing up her pistol when the guy reversed. A heavy paw clamped down on Geren's gun hand, driving the muzzle toward the ground.

Geren folded her legs, letting the big man support her weight for a moment. As he staggered, she straightened her legs again. A hard double stomp smashed into the guy's foot, and she was rewarded with the sound of snapping bone.

The big man grappling with her responded with an open-handed swat that caught her on her ear. Geren's head rolled, eyes jerking in her skull from the impact.

"Little bitch," the Egyptian growled.

Geren wrapped one of her legs around the staggering giant's ankle and twisted her body. Both of them went tumbling into the grass next to the path. As they fell, Geren managed to maneuver herself so her forearm came crashing down like a guillotine blade on her enemy's throat. He coughed and sputtered, spit drooling from one corner of his mouth. Geren sneered and gave his eyes a hard rake with the denim wrapped around her forearm. He screeched in pain, finally releasing Geren's wrist.

She swung the gun and hammered the steel frame hard into the temple of the man, bone cracking as she made contact. Brain damage or death was the result, and Geren didn't care whose side this goon was on. He was part of the same force that slaughtered Anwar, and she hoped that he lived with severe head trauma.

She wasn't going to stick around to find out his medical prognosis. A blast of gunfire came chasing after her, kicking up divots of sod. Geren got up and poured on the speed, racing toward the street when a green sport coupé came skidding to a halt. More players were entering the dangerous game of hunting Tera Geren.

She swore to herself she'd give as well as she got. Geren brought up her Helwan when a familiar face stared at her.

"Get in!" Bolan growled. "And get down." Muzzle-flashes flickered from the park, bullets pinging against the door.

Geren didn't have to be told twice, and she scrambled into the vehicle. Bolan gunned the engine, and the Audi picked up speed, swerving past automobiles. He swung the car into oncoming traffic in order to get cover against the gunmen in the park.

Geren poked her head up and saw a squirming form being manhandled into the back of a van by a half dozen struggling Egyptians.

"Brandon!" Geren said. "It's Alex!"

Bolan swerved back into the proper lane and screeched to a halt.

"You drive," he told her.

"What's your plan?"

Bolan shoved a Desert Eagle into her hands. "I'm going to try to get Alex back. Keep the engine running and ward off anyone who gets too curious."

With that, he was gone.

BOLAN, BERETTA DRAWN, raced toward the black van that Tera Geren said Alex Kalid was in. Every step, he kicked himself for going on a fool's errand. He could easily get them both killed, but the Executioner long ago vowed that he would never leave a fellow soldier in enemy hands.

The van started up and a blazing scythe of autofire raked toward him. Bolan dived to the sidewalk, his clothes and skin tearing as he hit the ground.

Gunfire kept dogging at his heels and Bolan rolled madly, bringing up the Beretta in a furious flurry of 9 mm fire. Bullets slashed along the side of the van and it swerved hard, peeling off down a side street. However, Bolan's fusillade struck true, and the gunman's rifle clattered to the street as the van violently swerved.

Bolan staggered to his feet.

Geren hit Reverse hard and brought the Audi back to where he could pour his battered form into the shotgun seat. "Let's go, soldier!"

"Move!" Bolan answered, piling in.

Geren showed how deft she was with a pair of good wheels, swinging the Audi down the side street before an on-coming truck blocked their path. Horns blared behind them, brakes squealing as they narrowly avoided becoming a squishy hood ornament. The side street was more like an alley, but Bolan could see the van in the distance. He pulled a spare magazine from his pocket and reloaded the Beretta. He pocketed the half-empty mag for later use.

"Don't you have anything bigger?" Geren asked, handing him back the Desert Eagle.

"Left it all behind in Lebanon," Bolan answered. "Get us closer, and I'll try to shoot out their tires."

Geren nodded and gunned the Audi, milking more speed from the little roadster. The van swerved right and onto a major six-lane street, delaying Bolan's return of fire. Traffic was chaotic, however, and the van was slowed by ancient trucks and cars, horses and camels.

"What kind of country lets goddamn camels on the road?" Geren asked in frustration, trying to get the Audi around a grunting dromedary.

"As long as they don't start a firefight with all these people around, we'll be…"

Bolan should have known better than to tempt the gods of war against him. The back door of the van was kicked open, and two burly Egyptians were raising Kalashnikovs.

Bolan leaned out the window, bringing up his Desert Eagle in a desperate race to get off the first shots.

Bolan hit the trigger first, and one gunman's face and chest were obscured by sprays of gore from twin .44 Magnum hits. The killer went crashing back into the van while his partner sprayed a long burst at the Audi. Bolan winced as a hot round punched through the windshield, grazing his hip.

Half-exposed, Bolan wasn't going to remain a sitting duck for long and he swung around the Desert Eagle. Two more .44 Magnum talons clawed apart the torso of the second rifleman, and Bolan sank back into the car. Blood was already running down the leg of his jeans, and he looked at Geren who was wiping blood from her face.

"Tera?"

"Glass cut my forehead. No bullet wounds," she responded tersely. "This job sucks."

The gunfire had its intended effect, however, and cars and livestock were suddenly veering to make room for the growling black van. Geren started forward again when a flock of sheep suddenly came racing in front of the car. She hit at least one before she could apply the brakes. A herder shouted at them, waving his stick.

"I think I killed a sheep," Geren said, her voice quavering.

"Get it together," Bolan answered.

"I killed one sheep, and the rest are too much to drive over or through and that van's getting away!" Geren shouted. She leaned out her window and opened fire, trying to track the speeding vehicle with her pistol. Bolan knew it was useless, but he, too, opened fire, knowing the range was too great. The van swerved away, disappearing into the maze that was Cairo. Sheep parted crazily, but other vehicles were filling in the road ahead of them.

One camel lazily clopped in front of them, droppings plopping behind it and covering the road in front of them as Geren tried to get the Audi to do more than inch forward.

The sheepherder had been scared off by the irate little woman with the 9 mm gun. Bolan looked her over.

"I couldn't have driven through this mess either," he said.

"Camel shit," Geren answered. "That's all we're left with here."

14

J. R. Rust didn't hide the MAC-10 as he watched the Audi pull up in front of the room. A dent in the front and bullet holes marking the side showed that enemy action had occurred. Apparently the big soldier's instincts were right, judging by the looks of the incoming survivors. He watched as only two people exited the car, worn and haggard.

"Rough day at the office?" Rust asked.

"Enough with the wisecracks. Anwar was murdered. Alex was kidnapped," Bolan said.

"Kidnapped? Why?" Rust asked.

"To find out what we know about this conspiracy," Bolan answered, moving to the bed and sitting. "That's not much, and we're on a countdown now."

"So finding Mr. Tank Dealer is top priority," Rust said. "I'm narrowing it down among—"

"We find Tofo."

Rust felt himself cut off cold. Geren was deadly serious.

"He's going to be tougher to find. This guy actually had hard contact with you," Rust said.

"I don't give a crap," Geren replied. "Tofo is the name we have, and we're going to pull Alex's location out of him, shred by shred."

Rust looked at Bolan, who showed all his mileage on his face. The soldier nodded.

"You two are insane. Tofo is a cold-blooded murderer. And a professional. He's not going to stick around for you to look him up for a friendly chat," Rust told them.

"Give me what you know. It's time to start shaking some cages here," Bolan answered. "They're using Muslim Brotherhood agents too. I can lean on them, make them squeal if you give us a few locations."

"You don't speak enough Arabic," Rust said.

"I do," Geren said.

"Is THAT YOU, J.R.?" Major Jake Marlboro asked over the cell phone.

"No, it's Larry Hagman. Have you seen my Jeannie?"

"Funny. What do you need?"

Rust tried to weigh his request and just let slip. He wasn't usually so blunt, but subtlety in getting information from his Cairo contacts wasn't a luxury he could afford.

"I've got a man missing. He's been grabbed by the Muslim Brotherhood."

"I'm sorry. We'll send flowers."

"Fuck that, Jake," Rust said.

"Listen, we hear things at embassy security about the Brotherhood. They're bad news. They'll pull a guy's eyeball out just so they can watch him squirm and bleed. Your guy's a write-off."

"I don't have a pen and paper big enough to write him off. I need a handle. A location. A hangout. Anything."

"J.R., you're not going to bully or intimidate the Brotherhood into giving up one of their own."

"No, I'm not, but I know someone who will."

There was silence on the line as Marlboro chewed over his choice of response. "Who do you have?"

"If I told you, I'd have to kill you, and we're already burying one buddy."

"That buddy wouldn't happen to be part of Unit 777, would he? A guy gone AWOL?"

Rust held his tongue. He, too, was stung at the loss of the brave, young Egyptian. "You have my handle? Or do I ask elsewhere?"

"If the Brotherhood finds out that we gave up one of their locations…"

"Quit pussyfooting, Jake."

"All right," he answered. The embassy Marine spilled all.

BOLAN WINCED AS GEREN finished taping his hip wound. His body was covered in various patches of tape. Antiseptic gel was squeezed over his scrapes and into the furrow a bullet had slashed through his flesh.

At any other time, Geren would have been amazed at the rippling muscles under the sleekness of his skin. He was supple and limber, despite a face that showed the toll of years she never wanted to see. It didn't detract from his handsomeness. In a way, the crisscross of old battle wounds added to his appeal as a man who kept going despite countless injuries. The bullet crease on Bolan's hip would be just another streak on the road map of his skin.

"So you slept with Alex?" Bolan asked her.

Geren leaned back. "I'm that obvious?"

"I recognized the brittleness in your voice when you were making J.R. back down," Bolan explained.

"You're not passing judgment?" Geren asked, slipping off the bed they were using as an impromptu first-aid station.

"I've been guilty of worse."

Geren's jaw dropped.

"We all have moments when we reach out to others," Bolan said, standing and pulling on a fresh pair of jeans.

"I'll understand if you want me to sit on the sidelines. I might not be thinking clearly," Geren said.

Bolan set his jaw firmly, regarding her. "You unraveled just for a little bit, but you recovered quickly."

Geren bent and fished under the bed, coming free with a case full of guns. She was trying to dismiss the image of Anwar's sad eyes burrowing into her soul. "Where did J.R. get this firepower?"

"We picked this dive for a reason," Bolan explained.

Rust entered the room. "Yeah. It's a safehouse. When we put operatives in the area, we try to set them here. Not too many tourist dollars go into a joint like this, so the Egyptian army doesn't place a group of squatters on hand. We have our own squatters here, and they keep a supply of specialized equipment."

Geren pulled out a MAC-10 and loaded it with a magazine of 9 mm manglers. "Especially if that specialty happens to be blowing people away?" She grabbed some spare magazines and put them on the bed, pulling out a hip pouch to carry them all in.

"A Glock." Geren picked out the polymer Austrian pistol. "I'll take this over these cheapo Helwans, thank you."

"My current gear is good enough. I will take that M-16 though," Bolan said.

"Here you go," Geren replied. "Isn't that long for indoor action?"

"You're right. Grab an M-16 for yourself, just in case, and hand me that MP-5."

"Too bad the M-16s don't have grenade launchers," Geren stated, complying with the big man's wishes.

Bolan checked the feel of the weapon against his shoulder, then slung it. "I'll make do. You have places for us to see, people to do, J.R.?"

"Perceptive as always, Striker."

"Great. Hold down the fort?" Bolan asked.

Rust nodded. "Just phone in your location."

"You got it."

Bolan regarded Geren with his steely gaze. "Ready to raise hell?"

"Let's turn this town on its ear," Geren snapped.

ALEX KALID FELT THE PAIN first. His whole body ached as he hung by his wrists. Chains dug into his forearms, and his chest was on fire as his own weight made it difficult to breathe. That difficulty had shocked him from unconsciousness, and he could feel his feet pushing, trying to keep him from strangling himself. His eyes opened and he saw a hawk-faced Egyptian man, rubbing his goateed chin. The face was familiar, and it took only a few more heartbeats to pump enough blood into his brain to give him the sentience to recognize Major Pedal Tofo.

"You have awakened, Sleeping Beauty," Tofo greeted him.

It took a few moments to register his surroundings. It was mostly dark, but a vat of coals glowed in one corner. The harsh light of a naked lightbulb rained down on the room, throwing things in stark contrast. They weren't alone. At least three men were visible, and Kalid wasn't sure who was behind him, but his back tingled with the presence of an unseen body.

Kalid looked down at his chest and realized it was bare. As he tried to shift position, he felt himself dangling, bare to the world.

"No wonder you called me Sleeping Beauty," Kalid answered. "You've seen perfection."

"Defiance? These men can peel the skin from your body for a week and leave you awake and screaming every moment of it," Tofo said, stepping closer.

"You want me to scream, keep breathing in my face," Kalid answered. "Ever hear of the concept called breath mint?"

The punch to the stomach came with sudden violence,

making him gag. Bile rose in his throat, and he teetered backward on the chains.

"What do you know?" Tofo asked.

Kalid caught the motion of Tofo's spin kick in time to tense up. The Egyptian's shin smashed hard into Kalid's tightened abdominal muscles, and he was left breathless a second time, tasting the acid of his own digestive juices in his nose. He breathed out heavily through his nostrils, making himself look like he was suffering more than he was.

Tofo leaned in close again. He brought up his knee, catching Kalid in the crotch.

This time, Kalid vomited, chunks of his last meal pouring over his lower lip and spilling onto his chest.

"This is going to be a very long, very bad day for you," Tofo whispered in his ear.

THE EXECUTIONER CHECKED the load on his machine pistol, then began a countdown with his fingers. Geren watched his hand while keeping an eye on their back trail. When Bolan's fingers descended into a fist, he swung around and opened the door to the back of the restaurant. Sunset was drawing a blanket of deep blue across the sky outside. By all rights, if the restaurant were legitimate, it should have been packed by now.

Instead, the two men in the kitchen, smoking lazily, jerked up with surprise at the sight of two armed people racing toward them. One of them reached for a knife while the other clawed for a pistol tucked into his waistband.

Bolan breathed an internal sigh of relief—this was a legitimate hardsite. He directed his MP-5 toward the guy attempting a fast-draw. The machine pistol burped as Parabellum rounds exited the foot-long Gem-Tech suppressor. The handgunner did more than burp as his body was kicked across a tabletop of pots and pans, metal clamoring and clanging on the floor before he crashed atop them.

The other figure was a blur of motion, knife slashing toward Bolan's chest. The Executioner was barely able to bring up the frame of his machine pistol to block the descending edge, metal singing off metal. The point bounced, but not far enough to spare Bolan a wicked welt along the back of his hand. Shock made him drop the weapon, only its sling keeping him from losing it.

The knife fighter took another step forward and Bolan was ready to block and counterattack when Geren screamed, "Drop!"

Bolan instinctively curled up into a ball, halving his height. The knife fighter's slash missed him, but not by much as he felt his hair brushed by the razor edge of the butcher knife. More of the strangled burping sounds filled the kitchen, blood raining down on Bolan's head and back. He looked up, seeing the Egyptian knife man staggering backward, most of his chest and face gone. He seemed to hang for a moment, then the strings of life that kept his body erect let go, spilling the marionette to the floor.

"It's about time you got out of my line of fire," Geren told Bolan. "You okay?"

Bolan looked at his hand, grimaced, and then looked over his machine pistol to see if it was in operating condition.

"You're bleeding again."

"It's far from my heart," Bolan answered. "Watch the door. We lost the element of surprise."

Geren nodded, and Bolan drew a roll of duct tape. Wiping off most of the blood with a dish towel, he ripped a tattered rag loose, packed it over the cut and taped down the improvised pressure pad. Flexing his fingers for a moment, he decided he passed the test of manual dexterity.

A couple of tentative voices called through the waiter swing doors.

"Ready?" Geren asked.

Bolan nodded. "I've wasted enough time."

"No rest for the wicked."

No rest, no mercy and nowhere to hide, Bolan thought, shouldering from the kitchen to the dining area, MP-5 up and tracking.

15

The scene as Mack Bolan plunged into the restaurant's main dining area was one he was familiar with from countless such raids, the particulars changed only due to decor and nation. Four men, armed with rifles, were still reacting to their impression that something was wrong.

Even with a moment's advance warning, the gunmen in the room were still caught off guard by the explosion of flesh that hammered through the door, 9 mm autobursts ripping from the submachine gun. Bolan wasn't aiming for flesh, only for disorientation. Tabletops exploded as he swept them while he kept two steps ahead of any possible reactive fire.

One step behind him, moving at the same breakneck pace, was Tera Geren, her MAC-10 making a sound like an extended rip roar as the weapon cycled through the remains of its magazine. The two warriors had crossed half the restaurant, getting behind the cover of a buffet made of heavy oak. Finally the enemy started opening up, but by then, the thick buffet table absorbed the return autofire like a sponge, letting none through to harm Bolan or Geren.

Bolan reached into his combat harness and pulled a canister from one pouch, then showed Geren the label. He pulled the pin, sailing the bomb over the buffet.

Geren and Bolan both opened their mouths to equalize the pressure in their eardrums just as the restaurant sounded like

Thor himself was striking the Earth. The blazing flash of the stun-shock grenade flickered brightly, but not enough to impair Bolan's vision. They popped up and spotted their adversaries, sprawled dazedly.

"Be gentle with them," Bolan advised Geren, bounding to the stairwell that led to the second floor.

Halfway up, he heard grunts of pain as Geren kicked and herded the blinded and deafened terrorists into one corner of the room. Reloading on the run, Bolan shook his head.

Reaching the first landing, HK cocked and primed, he looked up in time to spot a couple of newcomers to the fight. They were close, and Bolan could see clearly down the barrels of their submachine guns. At barely ten feet, Bolan had no tricks to take the men alive, so he gave up more potential prisoners, bringing up the MP-5. The sizzling little machine pistol hissed out a slaughtering wave of slugs that ripped a bloody swath through the two men.

Without stopping, the Executioner vaulted their lifeless forms before they came completely to a halt, landing in a half crouch, scanning the second story of the restaurant. Down the hall, a gun barked, belching missiles at him one at a time.

Bolan hit the ground with a grunt, slugs whizzing over his head. It took a moment for realization to kick in. Someone else had a Desert Eagle, and they were hammering heavyweight hollowpoints at him. A .44 Magnum round gouged out a massive scratch in the floor near Bolan's face and he threw himself hard to one side, barely avoiding the next geyser of splinters from the hardwood floor. He ripped off a couple of bursts, and lunged to the other side of the hall on instinct. A chunk of plaster blew out of the wall where his head had been.

Even as he was cursing the irony of the situation, Bolan was raking the doorway with his MP-5, bullets hammering away mercilessly at the barricaded opponent.

The enemy fire stopped, and Bolan let the machine pistol drop on its sling, smoothly drawing his own Desert Eagle to replace the emptied weapon. He advanced slowly, fully aware that each step might be his last.

The sound of a magazine being rammed home and the slide being racked on a big pistol brought that fact into stark reality, and Bolan charged forward, cutting the distance between himself and the doorway. The terrorist with the Desert Eagle swung around again, bringing up the big .44 when Bolan was right in his face, left forearm deflecting the gun skyward. The Executioner swung around the muzzle of his own weapon, the heavy, reinforced barrel striking jawbone solidly.

The terrorist's head bounced off the doorjamb. The impact forced a reflexive trigger pull, the muzzle-blast crashing across the Executioner's senses like the wrath of God. Blind and deaf for an instant, Bolan didn't give up his fight. With a powerful surge of one leg, he kneed the terrorist between his legs and grabbed a fistful of hair. With a savage twist, he sidestepped across the hall, his shoulder striking a wall. Bolan kept dragging his opponent headfirst to meet the plaster, feeling hair rip free in his hands. The soldier yanked hard again, feeling more scalp tear away with the second skull-bash.

A fist arced weakly into Bolan's rock-hard stomach. He took the hit and stomped his combat boot hard on the man's instep. His vision was clearing quickly. Bolan twisted and slashed his elbow into the neck of the Muslim Brotherhood gunman like an ax.

The terrorist finally collapsed to the ground.

"Drop the guns!" a voice called from one side.

Bolan blinked away the last of the flash hovering in his eyes. He was aware of a slender figure aiming a weapon at him.

"I said drop the guns!" she shouted.

Bolan looked at her, letting the Desert Eagle fall to the floor. "Why didn't you shoot when you had the chance?"

The gun in the young girl's hands shook. "The other guns too."

"I'm not here to kill you. I'm here looking for answers."

"What about the others?" she asked.

"They were going to kill me."

The gun was wavering now. Bolan took a step forward. The muzzle exploded, but the shot was far and wide, and the girl, in pure shock, took a step back, nearly dropping the weapon. Instead, the Executioner lunged in and chopped the weapon from her shaking fingers.

"You, however, weren't," Bolan told the girl as she massaged her shocked hand.

"What do you want?"

"The Muslim Brotherhood took a friend of mine. I want to know where he is."

"I don't know."

Bolan looked the young woman up and down, then bent, picking up her weapon. "I didn't think you did."

The girl nodded at the boneless lump, face leaking blood into the carpeting. "He knows."

"He's not looking too talkative," Bolan said. "But you are."

"Because I am not of the Brotherhood. I don't have the right parts to be a brother. Even if I did, I wouldn't care except that they have a knife to my throat," she said.

"But I'm still stuck with no information to stop these bastards," Bolan growled.

"He has a phone. It records numbers."

Mack Bolan smiled.

TERA GEREN HUNG ON TO the whirlwind as they followed the list of phone numbers they got from the Muslim Brotherhood restaurant. It was at the second stop that they saw the familiar, bullet-pocked black van. It was parked in front of a small house, and the majority of the damage was being covered with tape as Bolan and Geren pulled up in the Audi. The guy doing the bodywork started to reach for his gun, but Geren was out of the car, swinging the stock of her MAC-10 into the man's face. His head bounced off the back of the van, and Geren nailed him in the stomach with the stock again. He crumpled to the ground.

Bolan was moving to the front door. He stopped halfway. He drew and primed two stun-shock grenades from his harness and whipped them like major league fastballs through the front window of the little house. Glass shattered instants before the atmosphere inside rocked with thunder and light.

Geren was hot on the Executioner's heels as they burst through the front door.

They hit the house fast and hard. Bolan swept the side of the hallway away from the living room with the unblinking eye of his machine pistol while Geren made an immediate hook to get to the men who'd taken the full force of the shock grenades. One man was starting to move and she gave him a full-force punt right under his chin, feeling his jaw break from the toe of her steel-reinforced boot. The guy flopped like a landed fish and stopped squirming on his back, eyes half open but unfocused.

"Nobody else make a move!" Geren shouted. She fired off a burst that landed between the splayed legs of one stunned Egyptian, and he scurried back to the wall.

"Your van was used to take my man," she continued. "I have twenty-seven shots. There's only five of you, so I can take my time killing you."

A blast of autofire sounded to one side, but she wasn't distracted. The man she knew as Colonel Brandon Stone was ripping through the house on a rampage. Nobody would come to blindside her. Suppressed submachine-gun fire answered the blast, and a body hit the floor heavily.

"Your backup is dead," Geren announced. "You're next."

"Go to hell, Jew," one Egyptian began before his knee exploded into a volcano of bone and blood. He twisted and screamed. Geren stomped on the shattered joint, ramming the burning muzzle of her suppressor into his neck. All she could think of was Alex Kalid, and what was being done to him right then. This time, she wasn't holding back on her anger. She needed every ounce of force she could get to convince these men that she meant business.

She accepted that things were going to get bloody.

"Shut the hell up," Geren ordered. "I don't care how slow you die. And I have my knife set to take your nuts off and feed them to a pig."

Fear now showed on the faces of the men present, even before the Executioner's tall, impassive frame blocked the light from the hallway.

"Is everything under control here?" Bolan asked.

"Take a hike. I got me some pigs to castrate," Geren said. She let the machine pistol drop on its sling, drawing out the knife that he'd loaned to her.

Eleven gleaming inches of steel shone in the setting sunlight. Geren saw the reflection of the terrified eyes of her kneecap victim. "You want to be first?" she asked.

"You're bluffing!" the Egyptian spoke.

Geren shrugged and slashed along his groin, slicing his pants open. Hot urine sprayed as if it were coming from a firehose, and she rammed his head into the wall, savagely hammering him on the face with the handle of the knife. Cheekbones broke like eggshells. Ruined features leaked blood into a mask over his face and the terrorist curled up, legs crossed, lungs heaving with sobs of terror.

She stepped back, sneering, then stepped to the next

stunned terrorist, wiping the blood from her knife. As furious she was, she was terrified by how easily she was resorting to pure barbarism. Mentally, she was putting on the brakes to keep from enjoying the suffering from others. She wanted to tear the balls off all of these bastards. She grabbed the guy's ear. "You're next?" she asked.

Terrified eyes looked at the pulpy-faced mess in the middle of the floor. The nearly foot-long blade hadn't even been used to cut, and it had reduced the poor man to a broken lump of a weakling.

"I asked you..." Geren pressed the knife edge to the guy's cheek. "You're next?"

"We handed him off to Major Tofo," the man whispered, tears flowing down his cheeks.

"Where? Where's he hiding?" Geren asked.

"Tofo..."

"If you're afraid he'll kill you, just remember who's got the knife and who's the fillet."

The Egyptian swallowed hard, then sang.

"How did you learn about this mountain bunker?" Rust asked as Bolan and Geren finished cleaning up from their journey through Cairo.

"We cut out the small talk," Geren said. "M-16s alone aren't going to win a mountain assault."

"We could use bunker-buster rounds," Bolan stated. "But we want to get Alex back."

"They transported him there that quick?" Rust asked. "It still sounds like bullshit. No way they'd tell the Muslim Brotherhood about a secret Egyptian military installation."

"It's not Egyptian military, though," Bolan explained. "It's Muslim Brotherhood. And they're sharing the facilities with General Idel."

"General Idel?"

"That name rings a bell with you?" Geren asked.

"His father was killed when the Israelis made their press to take the Suez Canal," Rust answered. "He was a kid at the time. He joined the army as soon as he could. Since his daddy was army brass, he was put on the fast track to be an officer."

"All the while, he has a grudge against Israel," Geren said.

Rust nodded. "He is vocally a moderate."

"Like he's supposed to wave a sign that reads 'I'm secretly plotting with Hezbollah and the Muslim Brotherhood to smash the Jews'?'" Bolan asked.

"Point taken," Rust stated.

"So what do you have coming in for us?" Bolan asked.

"You'll get to survey the goodies when we get to the air-field. You are trained for HALO diving, aren't you?" Rust asked Geren.

"Better than you Yanks. Israeli paratrooper training is the best in the world," she answered.

"Not a little ethnocentric, is she?" Rust asked.

Geren's face reddened. "Listen, I just sliced a guy's groin to get information about where Alex is. I'm sick and tired of dicking around."

"All right. We're in motion," Rust said, heading to the door.

Rust saw Bolan put an arm on Geren's shoulder, and she nodded as he whispered softly to her. He wasn't able to hear what was being said.

When she looked up, her frustration was gone.

Only steel remained, a steel matching the big soldier's.

16

Kalid was breathless. The weight of his body against his restrained arms was cutting off the air to his lungs. As he struggled to straighten, he backed against the sizzling heat of a hot pipe pressed behind him. As long as he sagged, he didn't cook, but he suffocated. If he pulled himself up enough to breathe, he felt his flesh blistering even deeper in contact with the pipe.

Tofo sat across from him, smoking a cigarette, which made breathing even more difficult. His gaze never left the American. An evil smirk crossed his lips.

"Half Egyptian, half Cuban. And working for the Americans?" Tofo asked.

Kalid coughed. "What are you talking about?"

"Ahman, he recognized your accent. Cuban."

Tofo laughed and strode up, stubbing out his cigarette in Kalid's armpit. The jumble of nerves and sensitive skin there exploded in warnings of pain and damage. Tears poured down his cheeks, but he kept his teeth crushed together.

"This would go so much easier if you just told me what you knew about the operation, Alessandro Johnson." Tofo's voice wafted forward to his ears.

"We know enough to shut you down, shithead," Kalid answered.

"Really? I'd like specifics," Tofo said. "Then I could end this quickly."

"I gotta laugh," Kalid croaked. He tried to punctuate his statement with a laugh, but it only came out as slight coughing.

"Tell me," Tofo said. "What is funny?"

Kalid pushed back to breathe more, and he didn't feel the hot pipe. It had been moved. "I was feeling naked and vulnerable coming into Cairo without a weapon."

"Oh really?" Tofo asked. "And now?"

"You don't scare me," Kalid whispered. He tried to get his balance, but something hard hit the backs of his knees, and he was soon hanging straight down from his wrists. His shoulders felt like they were tearing.

"No?"

"You annoy me," Kalid growled. "You're a pathetic excuse for a human being."

"Keep talking, but steer the conversation toward something with an actual conclusion," Tofo ordered.

"You want my conclusion? I conclude that your mother sucks sheep dick," Kalid said.

Tofo swung the hot pipe, slamming it into Kalid's ribs. He'd put on a pair of insulated gloves to keep from burning himself on the heated metal. Kalid winced again. Another hard rap crashed off his rib cage. The third time he was just prodded with the pipe until he gurgled uncontrollably in agony. Reflexive convulsions gave way to inarticulate expression.

"Keep up your silence, boy. It won't be long before we undertake our plan, with or without forewarning about what you know," Tofo taunted. He brought a fresh cigarette to his lips and lit it.

"Kind of figured that," Kalid moaned.

"Do tell?"

"Israel is spreading itself to deal with whatever threat you can get the Hezbollah to pretend to be. Nitzana. Nahariyyah. Oh wait. That didn't happen, did it?" Kalid asked.

Tofo leaned in close. "You know about Nahariyyah?"

Tofo pressed the pipe between Kalid's legs, and he couldn't hold back his wail of agony anymore. He screamed, thrashing on his chains. The touch lasted for only a few seconds, but it felt like an eternity and the aftereffects stayed with him. He felt nausea boil up from his stomach, but running on empty, he only gagged helplessly.

"We're getting somewhere." Tofo cackled gleefully. "Sloppy of you, Mr. Johnson."

"Motherfucker...motherfucker...if I ever get out of these chains, I'm going to break your neck."

Tofo smiled and gave Kalid's chin a tap. "That's why I'm never letting you out of those chains."

Kalid coughed up some bile, fists clenching. He could taste his death.

WHEN TERA GEREN LOOKED at the airfield, she thought that they'd bought into a betrayal for certain. Four helicopters with squads of grim-faced men assembled.

"J.R.?" Geren said.

"Relax, they're here on my say-so," Rust answered. "I have some good relations."

A wiry man, with skin so brown it looked like shoe leather, stepped toward Bolan. "You are Colonel Brandon Stone?"

Bolan nodded.

"I am Major Atef Fesjad, Colonel Stone. Anwar told me some of what was going on," the wiry little man explained. "Then the American embassy contacted us at your friend Mr. Russel's request."

"Anwar contacted you?" Bolan asked.

"He sent me a secure message," Major Fesjad replied. "He had more notes on him when we picked up his body."

There was an uncomfortable silence.

"Someone has turned Egyptian against Egyptian, and Egypt against her allies, America and Israel. They murdered my nephew, and they got his fellow soldiers murdered in conflict with you," Fesjad stated. "Anything you need to protect our nation's fragile peace with Israel, it is yours."

Bolan put out his hand. "Thank you for letting us see this through to the end."

Geren let out her breath finally as the men of Unit 777 began an impromptu briefing with the Executioner.

"IT'LL BE ANOTHER FIFTEEN minutes before we're in our drop zone," Major Fesjad announced. "I still don't think that sending you in first, Colonel Stone—"

"Enough members of Unit 777 have died, Major," Bolan cut him off as the Westland Commando helicopter tore through the night sky. "I just need your men to set up a kill box until we can figure out what's going on."

"And then you start blowing stuff up," Fesjad answered.

"If it comes to that," Bolan promised. "Nobody gets out of there."

Fesjad gestured out the window to the AH-64 Apache that was keeping pace with the pair of Commandos and the big Russian-designed MI-8. The quartet of helicopters were keeping so close to the ground, the lead helicopter threatened to clog the windshields of the following helicopters with blowing sand.

They'd crossed the Gulf of Suez only minutes before. At the speeds the helicopters were moving, the relatively short distance between Cairo and the Sinai Peninsula's inner region was eaten up in less than half an hour. It made sense to the Executioner that their enemy would be nestled where Egypt had historically kept its copper and turquoise mines. Nearly eight thousand years earlier, settlers set up shop to begin mining precious metals. Bolan reckoned that over eight millennia, a lot of tunnels would have been carved into the mountainsides. Jebel El Tih, a massive, rocky plateau that bisected the mighty triangle of the Peninsula, was only minutes ahead.

This was the land where Moses had gotten lost for forty years, and if the wonders of satellite imagery hadn't been brought down from on high, it would have taken that long to find any trace of General Idel's hideout. Thermal imaging and radar had picked up some traces, based on what they got from the Muslim Brotherhood. It wasn't easy, and the computerized search ate vital time before the helicopters could take flight.

The Egyptians, Bolan and Geren were all prepared for the frigid plateau, dressed warmly against the frosty chill. From desert broil to near arctic tundra, the Executioner was set to fight to the end of this war wherever it took him.

Bolan glanced over to Geren, who was cradling a spare Colt M-4 assault rifle that Unit 777 brought along. It was no surprise to the Executioner that the Egyptian specialists were armed with American equipment. They trained with American forces, so using the same top of the line equipment was natural. Bolan knew that they were highly skilled and hardcore veteran fighters.

Bolan double-checked his weapon. It wasn't an act of distrust of the Egyptian special forces armorers. It was knowing that being intimate with each tool you carried into combat was the difference between life and death.

The MI-8 and one Commando swerved away as their Apache escort kept tight with them.

"Your drop-off point, Colonel," Fesjad told him. "Another ten minutes. The others are swinging around to close the box."

"Just make sure they keep well back. There's no telling what kind of antiaircraft General Idel has," Bolan warned.

"He doesn't have enough antiaircraft to keep me from seeing his operation put out of commission," Fesjad declared. "Good luck, Colonel Stone."

TOFO WASN'T HAPPY TO BE pulled away from toying with the captive. Still, when the boss called, business came before pleasure.

"How goes the interrogation?" General Idel asked, clenching his teeth around the soggy butt of a cigar.

"He knew about Nahariyyah."

"This isn't a surprise. Someone raised hell. Kazan never reported in, and my Lebanese sources have told me that they found him and nearly forty of his men slaughtered. Only one man escaped, and he said that the legendary al Askari himself descended upon them and killed them all brutally," Idel explained.

Tofo swallowed hard. "Al Askari? What about the tanks?"

"The Abrams we gave to the Hezbollah were all destroyed, as well as a good portion of their ammunition and fuel supplies," Idel grumbled. "If it was just one man, he certainly lives up to his legend."

"We have his lackey, though," Tofo reminded him. "We can figure out who al Askari is."

Idel glared. "Put a bullet through his head now. Al Askari was in Cairo as of two hours ago. Some even said he was chasing the very van that abducted your prisoner."

Tofo blanched.

"They were following the men you sent to take the American agents working with him," Idel added.

"They can't know about our complex," Tofo said, drawing back.

Idel's gaze smoldered.

"This is a Muslim Brotherhood stronghold. They know about it. We updated it on the sly, but it's still their territory!"

"So what do we do?" Tofo asked.

Idel snorted. "Prepare to repel invaders and let loose the dogs of war."

"We're launching?"

Idel smirked. "Go kill that useless prisoner. Now!"

KALID FELT THE EARTH shake as big, fast-moving engines pushed something outside. He couldn't be sure of what it was, but he wasn't taking the time to work out the exact details. He suspected it was the unmanned aerial vehicles that he and Tera had surmised were going to be used. The deadline was down, or perhaps the mystery man decided it was time to do his thing.

Tera. Her name danced across his mind like the fingers of a talented pianist in concert. He wondered how much their lovemaking was at fault for his being captured, but he cast aside that thought.

Alone, Kalid had the chance to try to get off the hook that held his chains. His whole body hurt like hell, and he was very weak. He got his feet under him and breathed deeply, concentrating. He figured help had to be on the way, otherwise the bad guys wouldn't be panicking.

He kicked off the ground without thinking, without giving his body time to react to the pain and effort. Arms yanking hard, he swung himself up and felt his feet impact with a support strut over his head. For the first time he could see what was above him. The roof of some sort of shack, held up with a couple thick beams of wood. Around him were crates of equipment and a table covered with tools that he figured Tofo would get around to sooner or later.

Kalid took it all in swiftly, then concentrated on getting his legs up and wrapped over the top of the wooden beam he was hanging from. The chains clinked with his effort, but he was more concerned by the agony in his shoulders and across his back. All of his weight was piling atop the already stressed out muscles as he worked to get his long, lean legs up and over. Finally, folding his knees over the support beam, his entire body quivered with thanks.

"One bit down, a whole bunch to go," Kalid whispered. He folded himself to reach the hook that he was hanging from. With one hand grasping the iron hook, he began working the chains over. His hands and forearms were slick with blood. The iron coils cut into his flesh, but he kept going. Links of chain barked against his knuckles until finally, he'd loosed the lot from the hook.

Kalid straightened and held his hands below his head, releasing the grip his legs had on the beam. Gravity took over and he hit the floor on his hands and knees, the concrete shredding skin where he hit hard.

They hadn't even bothered with manacles. The chains, simply knotted, were easy to shrug out of. He got them off his wrists but kept them well in hand. He was naked, but at least he had a weapon. It was an old, simple weapon, which wouldn't stop an AK-47-toting killer at thirty feet, but if anyone came in, they were going to catch some hell.

It was the least that Kalid could do to give back to the bastards who had tortured him.

BOLAN AND GEREN WERE climbing the mountainside when the roar of launching aircraft filled the air. Bolan looked up and saw the familiar cruise-missile shape of drones ripping out of the side of the mountain in a salvo, tearing off and swerving northeast.

Toward Israel.

"We're too late," Geren gasped.

"They're not supersonic. We've got to move quickly to stop them, but we can do it," Bolan said, putting his strength into crawling up toward the shelf carved out of the mountainside. The launches were almost finished, and the heat coming off their engines and the buffeting winds as they passed forced the soldier to dig in even harder to hold on.

Finally the last unmanned drone was gone. Bolan wondered if Fesjad would assign anyone to try to intercept the unmanned drones. He didn't want to break radio silence this close to their goal. He trusted the Unit 777 commander.

The drones had flashed past his vision too quickly in the dark for Bolan to get a decent look at them. He had counted around two dozen, but the winds kicked up by the tail rotors forced him to look away or blink, so it could have been twenty-five or thirty drones. Either way, he dreaded knowing what their payloads were. He'd seen mock-ups of remote drones used for biochemical warfare at Stony Man Farm.

Bolan hauled himself onto the flat rock, silenced M-4 sweeping the darkness. Geren tucked in behind him.

"This is a lot bigger than a mine entrance," Geren said.

Bolan looked around the hewn mouth to the cave. Now that the launching drones were long gone, the chill winds once more whipped the wall of the plateau. "I think this place has been under a lot of reconstruction. At least a couple centuries worth of work."

Geren looked up and down the wall they were against. "I like your style."

"What do you mean?"

"You don't waste any time," Geren said.

"Quick and quiet," Bolan cautioned, looking into the cave. He shouldered the M-4, clicking on the infrared illuminator atop the barrel of the compact assault rifle. His rifle's scope showed the inside of the cave in an eerie green as the invisible waves reflected off the targets they hit. Since the scope was not light amplification, he wasn't blinded by the small utility lights scattered throughout the interior of the mine entrance.

Soldiers moved with a purpose, spreading out, their rifles at the ready.

They were expecting trouble, either having detected the helicopter flight as it passed over the blasted lunar landscape of the sands leading up to the plateau, or they knew from Bolan's raids in Cairo that trouble was coming. From their reaction, the whole base had been put on full alert. He examined their weapons through the scopes, but the forces of General Idel weren't equipped with night vision. He wasn't splaying a suicidal beacon across them, pinpointing his position behind the infrared spotlight on his rifle.

"They know we're here," he whispered to Geren. "Or that we're on our way."

The Israeli woman nodded and slung her rifle tight across her shoulders. "Tofo just showed up. He's moving under their cover toward one of the sheds at the far end of this level."

Bolan nodded. "I'll say hello to them. You intercept Tofo."

Geren smirked. "I was just going to ask. Be careful."

"If I were careful, I wouldn't be taking on a mountain full of madmen by myself," Bolan replied.

He opened up, sweeping the cavern with the silenced M-4, soldiers screaming as swift, quiet bolts of death burst through them.

17

"What the hell is that?" Nateg asked as he gripped the controls of the idling AH-64 Apache. The sight of nearly thirty soaring darts tearing from the side of the Jebel El Tih took him totally by surprise. The big, dark-skinned Egyptian pilot looked at his co-pilot and gunner, a light-eyed wolf of a man he'd known for years. "Cruise missiles?"

"No," Ekan answered gruffly. "Unmanned drones. Can't tell what kind for sure, but we've got to do something."

Nateg shook his head. "What about the unit?"

Ekan could see Nateg's eyes following the departing drones. There was a slim chance that the pair could do anything at all.

"This is Deathbird to Nova, Deathbird to Nova. Major, we have to do something to intercept those things," Ekan radioed.

"That's a positive," Major Fesjad answered. Nateg heard him clearly. "We're here to stop a war with Israel, and those things could be the spark."

"Do it," Ekan said to the pilot.

Nateg pulled up on the cyclic, throttling the gas turbine engines to their utmost. The Apache shot into the air like a rocket, at well over 2000 feet per minute. Not the fastest of helicopters, it had an amazingly agile climb rate, and the Egyptian pilot thrust the gunship along.

"Ekan, do you have anything on those things?" Nateg asked.

"They're Predators," he answered as he swept them with

the Forward Looking Infrared cameras of the skyship. "And they're in dash mode. They're doing at least 220 kilometers per hour."

"They have the jump on us, but we can catch up," Nateg told Ekan.

The wolfish gunner looked at his old friend, then gave him a small salute. "Do it. We've got a war to prevent!"

TERA GEREN RACED ALONG, keeping one step ahead of a cloud of gunfire that was divided between taking her down and catching the tall man in black who was raining devastation on the improvised aircraft hangar. If she hadn't been running for her life, she would have admitted that using the mouth of the mine as a launch point for unmanned drones was a brilliant maneuver.

Since the craft were being used on a fire-and-forget basis, there would be no need to land them safely. The drone controllers wouldn't need to thread the needle, just finish their job then send the unmanned vehicles crashing into the sand like lawn darts.

Geren launched herself and hit the ground like a lawn dart herself. She landed behind a heavy crate that absorbed a sudden hailstorm of autofire. Coming up with her M-4, she returned fire, focusing on Kalashnikov muzzle-flashes, taking out two gunners before diving behind cover again.

More gunfire ripped and tore the air over her head, hungrily seeking flesh and only impacting on stone. A round bounced and nicked her calf. She winced as her black BDU pants swiftly began soaking with her blood. She ignored it and crawled along. Tofo was crouched in front of a shed, one-fisting an Uzi like something out of an action movie, sweeping the mouth of the cavern.

Geren brought up her M-4 and ripped out a short burst,

but was too slow. Tofo moved to cover instants before her bullets struck.

An arm reached up and over a stack of tires piled outside the shed, Uzi in fist, and began sweeping the ground with 9 mm slugs. Geren retreated, curling up as bullets tore after her. Dust flew all over her, but the only injuries she got were stings on her cheeks from where chips of flying stone struck her. Tofo withdrew his Uzi and ran to the door of the shed. Geren tried to catch him with a hail of M-4 fire before he escaped to harm Alex Kalid.

MAJOR TOFO DIVED THROUGH the door, bullets seeking his flesh but finding only unfeeling wood. His Uzi was empty, and he realized how close to death he'd just come.

That's when he heard the singing of steel in the air and ducked under a ribbon of crimson-tinted silver that would have taken his head off. Instead, the chain whip smashed hard into the doorjamb, cracking wood in a sickening crunch. Knowing his head could have been burst like an overripe melon spurred Tofo into action, swinging the Uzi toward his attacker. It was pure instinct, and he pulled the trigger without any effect.

A savage, naked figure grabbed the Uzi with both hands, driving it skyward. A long, lean leg hit Tofo in the groin, but the Egyptian renegade twisted his hip, catching the knee on his thigh. Tofo pulled down with both hands on the automatic weapon, yanking the taller man off balance and sending him skidding across the floor.

Alex Kalid landed on his shoulder, but rolled quickly to the balls of his feet, crouching, hands held like claws. He wished he hadn't dropped the chain when he went for the Uzi, but since the weapon didn't show any sign of being loaded, he felt some solace that he wouldn't die naked, plugged with a belly full of lead.

He'd sell his life only after he had no more enemies to kill.

Kalid lunged, his whole body stretching like that of a great cat. His clawed fingers bypassed the swatting Uzi's frame and clutched Tofo's uniform. His full weight threw the Egyptian rogue back against a crate that snapped under their impact. Tofo brought the Uzi around again, but instead of hitting Kalid in the head, the metal bounced off his burned and tender shoulder. The impact hurt like hell, but the ex-blacksuit hung on, leaning into the renegade. He freed up a hand and introduced the heel of his palm to Tofo's nose in an explosion of blood.

Tofo roared in anger and raked his fingers down Kalid's burned and battered back. Lightning flashed through the naked man's entire consciousness, but reduced to savagery, he was unhindered in his tactics by the pain. He screamed madly into the face of his foe.

Tofo stopped struggling, eyes wide in horror at Kalid's lunacy. Kalid's teeth bared and flashed, sinking into the bridge of the Egyptian's bloody nose, crunching through bone and cartilage before tearing free.

Tofo struck hard, punching Kalid away from him, holding his shattered face.

Kalid spit out a chunk of flesh.

The pair circled each other. Tofo took his hand away from his savaged face to pick up a pipe. Kalid stooped, scooping up the empty Uzi, holding it upside down like a side-handle baton.

Tofo swung first, and Kalid reacted with the Uzi, metal clanging on metal. The frame of the submachine gun took the impact of the pipe, sparing Kalid a broken arm. He lifted one foot and rammed it into Tofo's gut, pile driving him backward across the floor.

He was about to move in for the kill when the door slammed open, a body tumbling inward. Kalid whirled to meet the new threat but recognized the figure instantly. He glanced through the open door at a rifleman, then dived aside, barely avoiding a burst of autofire. Tera Geren came up from the floor, dodging toward cover as bullets perforated the wall.

Finally she came to a halt and was face-to-face with Tofo, looking stunned at the gaping hole in his nose.

Tofo took advantage of her shock by grabbing the barrel of her rifle. The two of them wrestled, Geren struggling with the weight of the rifle as the stronger, deadlier Egyptian started to pry it loose from her grasp.

Getting both hands on the barrel, Tofo tried to pull the weapon free, but Geren let go, throwing her whole weight on top of the noseless terrorist, bringing both hands raking into his face. Her gloved fingers blunted her clawing attempt, but she still gouged the Egyptian's eyes, making them burn.

Tofo screamed and released the rifle, but smashed one fist against Geren's head. She went rolling, dazed, but still ready to fight.

Tofo blinked away the eye gouge, turning the rifle around so he could fire. Kalid leaped into the fray, bringing down the Uzi like a hammer. Tofo barely managed to block the swinging steel of the SMG with the body of his own weapon. That didn't prevent Kalid from straddling the grounded Egyptian.

Tofo didn't bother righting his weapon. Instead he fired off a punch into Kalid's much abused abdominal muscles. The naked man curled up over the fist, and the Egyptian grabbed a clump of hair. A boot flashed out of nowhere.

Tofo screamed as his forearm broke from the force of Geren's kick. Kalid brought the Uzi, barrel first, down into Tofo's chest, stabbing and beating, metal holding strong as bone and gristle crunched beneath it.

"Alex!" Geren shouted.

Kalid sagged. The Uzi had punched through Tofo's rib cage in a dozen places.

"Hi, baby, was traffic bad?" Kalid asked, still straddling the dead man. Blood smeared across his face, chest and hands, only barely covering his burn marks.

Geren looked at him, then choked back a sob. "Terrible. I ran over a sheep, and a camel shit in the road."

Kalid nodded. He threw his arms around her and they squeezed each other tight.

"COLONEL STONE, CAN YOU hear me?" the voice blasted, tinny in Bolan's earpiece. It was Major Fesjad, contacting him over the radio set that was plugged into his ear.

He couldn't put his full concentration on what was being said, devoting his efforts more toward laying down a hot and heavy stream of cover fire for Tera Geren. However, return fire was starting to cut too close to him. Bolan dodged sideways, avoiding a blast of bullets. He came up from the shoulder roll, M-4 tracking and blazing before he managed to get to the cover of the far wall of the cavern.

"I can hear you, but could you hold on a moment?" Bolan requested, crouching tightly behind cover. He pulled out a grenade, flipped out the cotter pin and tossed the bomb around the corner. It bounced four times before coming to a halt, a shattering explosion rocking the mine entrance. Dust showered from the old ceiling, but it held.

Bolan knew another earthshaker like that wouldn't be good for anyone's health.

"I got a moment," Bolan said. "The drones…"

"We're sending the Apache after them. I'm sorry for compromising the perimeter, but…" Fesjad spoke up.

Bolan ran the comparative speeds of the combat helicopter and the unmanned spy drones through his mind quickly. "That might be enough, but if we can hit the command-and-control center, that'll give your Apache even better odds."

"You're pinned down," Fesjad began. "Need help?"

"I don't want any indiscriminate fire," Bolan said.

"You won't get any. Tell us where not to shoot," Fesjad requested.

"There's a supply shack. Rear right corner of the cavern," Bolan replied. He gave the shed a burst of illumination from his M-4.

"Keep the illuminator on it," Fesjad said. There was the bark of an order, then suddenly the Westland Commando popped out of the darkness. Hovering off the lip of the mine entrance, the side of the machine came alive with flickering tongues of flame, a broadside of automatic fire ripping into the gaping maw of the mountain. The thunder was deafening, but Bolan kept his illuminator aimed at the shed that Geren had disappeared into moments ago.

The gunners aboard the Westland Commando were tracking their targets with savage precision. Bodies flopped about as M-60s and M-16s spit flaming death from their barrels.

The firestorm ended suddenly, and an eerie silence fell over the mine entrance.

"I'm going in, cover me," Bolan requested.

"We have your back. Wish we could land to give you more support," Fesjad responded.

"Negative...stay in place. You lose my transmitter, then you can come in, unless my partners make it out there, then nuke the damn mountainside."

There was silence on the other end as Bolan ate up the ground with long, loping strides. He reached the shed. "Is that clear?" he asked.

"That's clear, Colonel. But I'm not going to sacrifice you to appease your guilt," Fesjad said.

Bolan mulled it over for a moment. "This isn't about guilt.

If I'm dead, and my partners get to your helicopters, just drop whatever hell down the mine shafts and scoot. I don't need a grave, but I'm not looking to end up in one. Out."

The Executioner was ready to blitz on, but he had two people to find first.

TERA GEREN LOOKED UP AS the Executioner burst through the door of the shed. He looked at her, then at Kalid. Both of them were covered in blood.

"Striker!" Kalid said.

"Are you two hurt?" Bolan asked.

Kalid shook his head. "The blood belongs to Tofo."

Bolan looked at the battered corpse in the corner. He chucked his parka to Kalid. "This will partially cover you."

Geren began ripping off her parka as well. "He can wear mine as a kilt."

Kalid slipped Bolan's jacket over his shoulders and tied Geren's around his waist, moving it so only one hip was bared. He looked down at himself, then moved over to the corpse, pulling off the combat boots. A few grunts later, he was shod. "All right, let's finish this."

"No, you two get out to the helicopter and wait," Bolan said.

"I have two words for you, Colonel. 'Fuck' and 'that,'" Kalid said.

"I've heard of a commando assault, but doing it while going commando?" Bolan asked.

"I'll need a gun," Kalid said.

Bolan unsnapped his gunbelt, handing over the Desert Eagle and the spare magazine pouches attached to it. "Trade up to something bigger. And aim high. At least you can grab a pair of pants if possible."

The Executioner and his allies spun, heading out the door.

18

Nateg and Ekan kept the AH-64 hot on the tail of the swarm of drones. Ekan was busy scanning them, waiting for the powerful engines of the Apache to get them within dogfighting distance of the deadly sky darts. The powerful imaging lenses in the nose gear of the Apache were meant to enable pilots and gunners to lock on to targets miles distant and destroy them without the enemy even knowing they were there. Unfortunately, the air-to-air options of the nimble gunship were limited to the 30 mm cannon nestled under its sleek frame.

"Closing to firing range," Nateg said.

"The Predators have something on their underwing hard points. I can't tell what, yet," Ekan replied.

"Missiles? Those things can hold up to seven hundred pounds," Nateg said. "That's enough for some serious blockbuster action."

"The image isn't clear. I don't think they're Hellfire missiles, they just look like dumb bombs," Ekan noted. The wolf-faced gunner squinted, as if to increase the power of the Apache's technology.

Nateg checked his radar screen. "We're in range. Let's fire a few rounds and see what they're packing."

Ekan took the stick and keyed the M-230 chain gun into helmet control. Once he got the aiming reticle floating on his helmet's visor, he drifted it over one of the Predators. Even so, he held the stick, wanting some extra finesse. The chain gun's "true" aim and his helmet's aiming point were divergent for a moment, his hand and eye coordinating. Then he depressed the firing stud. It was a short press, less than half a second. Five rounds belted out of the 30 mm cannon.

Explosive shells slammed into the Predator. The Predator was meant for reconnaissance, not for slugging it out with other aircraft. The machine flew to pieces instantly.

As the Predator disintegrated in midair, one cylinder fell away from the side, tumbling toward the ground.

Ekan took that moment to lock on the object, and he fired a short burst at it.

The drum disintegrated with the explosive force of the single 30 mm round that did impact with it. Nothing happened except for a spray of mist filling the air.

Ekan felt his bowels tighten, and he looked at Nateg.

"Hell," Nateg grumbled. "Those drums are full of chemical weapons. Where did they get them?"

"Who knows? Syria? Maybe it's just pesticide. Either way, it's too dangerous to be let loose, come on!"

Ekan began sweeping the sky with the Apache's M-230, tearing another Predator in two before the flight broke up, swarming in all directions.

The drones were suddenly aware that an even nastier predator was among them.

BOLAN TOOK THE LEAD, M-4 tracking as they made their way along a metal catwalk. The mine entrance had a tunnel that hooked to the left and led to a shaft where the catwalk stretched out to take miners to a hydraulic lift. Getting on board would attract attention the trio didn't need. Bolan shouldered his M-4 and swept the lift's structure, looking for the bottom. Through the green haze of the rifle's scope, he saw a landing with a tunnel leading off of it, gunmen lining up, ready to respond to anyone coming down by way of the elevator.

"Got a plan?" Geren asked him. She, too, saw the gunners through her rifle's scope.

Kalid knelt, cradling a weapon from one of the dead fighters who had tried to guard the mine entrance. He'd paused to peel the pants off the body. They weren't too much of a mess, but they hung in tatters around his legs. He took the pause in the action to slice them into shorts.

"There's about five of them down there. I don't want to use a grenade," Bolan said. "It'll bring down the roof, even with just a stun-shock."

Bolan looked at the stairwell that wound in a tight circle behind the hydraulic lift. He didn't like that approach into the depths, as the clatter of boots on metal would alert anyone below. His blue eyes scanned the darkness till he spotted a winch hanging from the ceiling, ropes dangling. The winch itself was rusted and old, but the ropes were new, checkered yellow-and-green nylon gear. An alternate form of transportation, but still across the dreaded catwalks. Through the grating, he could spot the gunmen below, perched and ready to open fire on them.

"Give me your gun," Bolan ordered Kalid, handing him his M-4. "I need cover fire."

Kalid looked confused for a moment, but he exchanged ammunition with the big soldier. "You're not going to go swinging down there?"

Bolan wrapped the sling on the AK-47 around his forearm, gripping it tight in his right fist. "I'll have only one chance. If I blow it, fall back and destroy this place."

Before either of his allies could object, the Executioner snapped to his feet, racing across the catwalk. As soon as his boot struck metal, gunfire erupted from below. Bullets sparked on grating, and the dull rip roars of sound-suppressed assault rifles filled the air behind him as Geren and Kalid opened fire.

Bolan's boots struck solid stone as a booming hail of slugs clattered against the catwalk, pellets bouncing off the stone ceiling just behind him. There was a frantic, angry cry below. He recognized the boom as the roar of a grenade launcher firing a buckshot round. Acting like a titanic shotgun, it fired a fist-sized wad of pellets that could shred flesh in a cone of death two yards wide.

Only the speed of the Executioner kept him from ending up slashed into strip steak. With three more bounding steps, Bolan launched himself, left hand reaching out and snagging the rope dangling from the winch. Friction seared against his palm and fingers before his crush grip took over. Bolan's weight suddenly began threading the rope through the pulleys, and he sailed down, seemingly out of control.

He stiff-armed the AK-47 in his fist and opened fire, sweeping a blast of steel-cored slugs across the gunners who were trying to track him. They screamed and fell, bullets punching into them, only a few able to return fire, aiming too high to hit the rapidly descending angel of death.

Bolan struck the ground, knees bent, shock jarring him head to toe. He was on the ground with the two remaining gunners, one arm snagged in the winch's ropes, the other holding an empty assault rifle. One of the gunners brought his rifle to his shoulder, but pulled the trigger on an empty weapon while the second gunman snarled and charged, knowing his gun was also empty.

The charging gunman used the muzzle of his rifle as a spearhead, not sharp enough to pierce flesh. That wouldn't matter with enough speed and strength behind the thrust. Steel would still break bone and tear flesh with ridiculous ease. Bolan leaped to one side, riding the rope in a swing that carried him over his first foe, boots dancing him forward along the wall.

Coming down on the second rifleman, Bolan whipped the muzzle of his weapon across the guy's face, steel meeting flesh and parting it all the way to fragile bone. The second gunner staggered back, dropping his rifle and magazine.

The first Egyptian spun and jammed the stock of his rifle into the Executioner's stomach, folding him over. Bolan grunted with the impact, losing his footing and skidding as the ropes slid him along the floor. He tucked in his legs to avoid having them chopped by the merciless weight of wood and steel in his enemy's hands. Getting one foot under him, Bolan lashed out with his other, kicking the gunner in the belly and snapping the AK-47's buttstock into his jaw, driving him into the wall.

With two steps, Bolan got himself upright, but didn't enjoy that position for long. The torn-faced terrorist slammed into him, screaming and clawing. The Egyptian grabbed Bolan's rifle. The Executioner had miscalculated the tenacity and suddenness of his enemy, as well as miscalculating the grip that the winch ropes and the rifle sling had taken on his arms. The bloody-faced madman knotted up his fist and launched a pair of brutal strokes into Bolan's face before the big soldier put his foot down. Tarsal bones shattered under the Executioner's boot, stunning the Egyptian enough to set him up for a knee between the legs.

Freed of his second foe, Bolan hung on hard to the ropes, using them for leverage to kick the first of Idel's fighters in the chest, stopping him cold. He loosened his grasp on his weapon and clawed at his chest harness, whipping free his knife. With a swift and savage slash, he freed one hand, and, transferring the knife, freed his other arm from captivity.

The battered Egyptians regrouped from their momentary defeat. The two men closed in on Bolan, holding their rifles like clubs. They were coiled like spring steel, waiting for an opportunity. The Executioner faked a misstep, and the twin rifles whistled through the air, slashing at him.

Ducking, Bolan lunged to the left, the razor sharp tip of the knife slamming into the groin of the man with the torn face. Rising swiftly, Bolan lashed upward, drawing the blade through the abdominal cavity of the terrorist. Guts spilled out as Bolan pivoted, ramming a roundhouse kick into his other foe.

Bolan could feel ribs break against his combat boot. The rifleman dropped his weapon, but the Executioner moved in swiftly, driving the harsh ribbon of judgment deep into the terrorist's chest cavity. Within moments, the fight was over.

Geren and Kalid were only halfway down the metal staircase, and moving quickly.

"Striker," Kalid said.

"I'm okay. Just a few bumps and a little bit of a burn," Bolan answered.

He fed a fresh magazine into his rifle. "Let's get moving."

GENERAL NAHD IDEL SHOOK his head as he rushed to the command-and-control center. The blast doors were thick, and it would take a lot of power to cut through. That would give him at least some time to accomplish his plan, and perhaps even repel the attackers already on the scene.

Bodyguards raced alongside the general as he made his way into the massive complex with rows of computer tables devoted to the control of the unmanned drones.

A wall radar displayed the sudden appearance of three Egyptian military helicopters. Idel immediately took them for Unit 777 ships.

"Air defenses?" Idel asked.

"We're trying to get targeting locks, but their pilots are keeping too low. They're only showing up on radar for a moment, opening fire, then ducking back against the mountainside or over the lip of the plateau," a captain spoke up. "I'm surprised we haven't been hit with more firepower than just those three."

"Sir, we lost three drones already!" came a cry from one of the controllers. Idel looked over one of the pilots' shoulders. A camera on the Predator was picking up the deadly sharklike form of the Egyptian Apache gunship as it slashed among the Predators.

"Six drones down! We're trying evasive!"

"Send five back toward us. The rest go on to Egypt. Target the enemy helicopters," Idel ordered calmly. "Keep a few to occupy and harass the Apache, crash into it if you must. Ten of them must get to Israeli airspace!"

THE DRONES WERE GETTING harder to catch now that their pilots back at the base knew the Apache was among them. Still, Ekan was glad to have taken out a full fifth of the enemy force. Nateg kept the Apache diving and climbing, weaving among the enemy to avoid a midair collision, but also trying to keep the gunner from missing targets of opportunity.

"Damn!" Nateg said.

Ekan cast his gaze from his helmet's display and to the radar screen in his gunner's bay. Five of the Predators had swung off, trailing back southwest at full dash speed. Others were breaking off too, ten ripping off to the north while the rest continued swarming around the Apache.

The hunter was suddenly the prey as the Predators circled.

"We're screwed," Nateg growled.

"We have to break out and get those drones heading for Israel," Ekan stated. "You have to get us out past them."

"You always get me into these messes, Ekan."

The Apache's engines blasted at full power. "You'd better call back to the others, Ekan. Those drones are going to lay down some deadly winds when they get back home."

"I'm ahead of you," Ekan replied. "Deathbird to Nova. Deathbird to Nova, be advised! Five incoming bogies, armed with chemical weapons!"

"Nova to Deathbird. We read you. Their antiaircraft has proved ineffective against us. This might be their idea of a response," Major Fesjad answered.

"We're going to try to break free and go after the drones heading toward Israel," Ekan stated.

"Ekan, you might run out of fuel. If you crash there, we won't have any way of bringing you home," Fesjad warned.

"It's a slim chance, but what's two lives against a thousand or more?" Ekan asked.

"Be nice if you asked me first," Nateg said as he swung the Apache between two darting Predators, lunging after the flight that had torn off from the main group.

"I don't see you disengaging the pursuit," Ekan stated.

The Apache roared into the darkness, followed by a swarm of deadly sky darts intent on smashing it from the sky.

BOLAN WAS LEADING the charge when his earpiece squawked to life.

"Colonel Stone. The general has turned a portion of his sky force back toward us," Fesjad warned. "They're Predator UAVs, and they have improvised canisters of chemical weapons hooked under each wing. Pull back and we'll blow this place."

"How are your men faring against the other drones?" Bolan asked.

"They're hard-pressed, and ten slipped away from them," Fesjad explained. There was a heartbeat of silence. "You're not turning back."

"If we take out the command and control, we can give your helicopter crew a chance to knock out the Predators over empty desert," Bolan explained.

"I was right about the unmanned drones," Kalid said dejectedly.

"What's wrong with being right?" Geren asked him.

"The fact that Unit 777, a lot of Israelis and we are all going to get killed when they deliver their nerve agents," Kalid answered.

"A wise man once said believe three impossible things before breakfast," Bolan told Kalid. "Technically it's before breakfast, so let's go stop those missiles."

"Those aren't missiles," Kalid said.

"All the better. They're slower, which gives us more time," Bolan stated.

Four gunmen raced down one of the side tunnels, spilling out into the open. They were going to make a hasty turn, presumably heading for command and control. Warning sirens were already sounding, but the new tone of the alert only confirmed Fesjad's warning that the mine complex and the surrounding area was going to be hammered with gallons of nerve agents.

Spotting Bolan and his allies, the gunmen froze, giving them the advantage they needed. Rifles flashed and recoiled, spitting a fountain of lead into the quartet, chopping them out of the way.

Kalid knelt and began pulling grenades off the dead men, stuffing them into an improvised pouch. "Command and control is going to be protected at least against nerve gas. That means we're going to have to get through one hell of a thick door."

"Blasting might bring the mountain down on top of us," Geren said.

"If it does, maybe we'll be lucky and it'll get them. Besides, I can use the grenades to help focus my own explosives," Bolan countered.

Geren shook her head. "Join the Mossad, see the world, meet interesting people, blow up underground terrorist bases…"

"It is written that 'May you live in interesting times' is not a blessing, but a curse," Kalid said.

Geren stuck her tongue out at him in a combination of mock defiance and stress relief.

"Onward and downward," Bolan ordered.

19

Major Fesjad watched the skies as the Commando helicopter hovered at the mouth of the mine entrance. He glanced down to the mine, and then back up.

"Nova to Horn and Nomad. Disengage and return to Blackjack base," Fesjad ordered.

"Negative, Major. We're picking up too much radio interference. Repeat again on that order to turn chickenshit," Nomad's pilot spoke up.

Fesjad smiled at the loyalty of his men. "We're going to be expecting some deadly incoming fire in a few moments."

Nomad darted over an antiaircraft gunner's nest, sweeping it with a blistering assault. The nest was silenced, and the Commando whirled back toward cover as bullets trailed in the sky behind it.

Fesjad shouldered his M-16, targeting the gunner's nest. He milked out half his magazine when the M-60 next to him roared, following the tracers he laid down on the target. Bodies churned and disintegrated under the hail of combined small-arms fire.

"Colonel Stone needed us to close the killing box. Right now, the only ones who're likely to be killed in this box are us. Nomad and Horn, get your stupid tails out of here now!" Fesjad ordered.

"We're still not reading you, sir," Horn answered from the other side.

Fesjad grumbled. "Nobody's willing to back down in this fight."

"Not when that bastard killed our best people. Besides, you didn't say you were leaving," Nomad's pilot said.

"I'm seeing this one out for my nephew. You don't have to," Fesjad explained.

"Yes, we do, sir," Nomad's pilot replied.

NATEG ROLLED THE APACHE as a Predator swung past it, just missing slamming into one of the wing stubs. Despite being rolled at enormous centrifugal forces, Ekan hit the firing stud on the M-230 chain gun, the explosive bolts ripping the Predator into a thousand shreds. Fragments of the shattered drone came slapping against the cockpit of the helicopter, and the pilot found himself wrestling to keep the aircraft right after coming out of its barrel roll.

Ekan targeted a Predator that was sailing at the extreme of the Apache's range. It took a 20-round burst to finally blast it into ragged wreckage, dumping it out of the sky and into barren sands where the winds of the desert would scatter and neutralize its deadly cargo.

Nateg grunted, swerving as another drone nearly clipped the rotors of the Apache as it dived down and swung up, getting out of the way of Ekan's retaliatory fire. His eyes were torn between the radar, watching over both shoulders, and not driving the Apache into the ground like a giant bug against a windshield. "How much ammo are we counting?"

Ekan looked at his counter. "Three hundred and thirteen rounds left. Not a lot to work with. How about fuel?"

"The arrow's almost pointing at *E*. I think that means enough, but it's hard to tell with these American controls," Nateg said.

"It's dark, we're three hundred kilometers from Cairo, we have an empty tank of gas, we're almost out of ammo and we're about to crash-land in Israeli airspace while they're on full alert for bad guys coming from Egypt," Ekan stated.

"Another day of fun with us," Nateg growled. "Keep knocking out those Predators. I'll keep our buddies off our tail!"

IDEL LOOKED UP AS MORE of his men opened fire at the door to the command-and-control center. "Close that door!" he ordered.

"But we have men out there!" one of the sentries yelled.

Idel pulled his pistol, jaw tightening with rage until he thought it would snap. He put a bullet into the sentry. "Get that blast door closed! The drones are almost here. If anyone's still outside, may God have mercy on their souls!"

The metal bulkhead door swung shut, screams and curses cut off by the clang of the airtight seal closing. Idel shook his head in sympathy, then moved toward the communications center, holstering his pistol.

"I wish to use this by myself," he told the officer.

"Sir," the young man said, getting out of his chair.

"I also want total privacy. Clear an area for me," Idel said.

The general turned, knowing his men would follow his orders, the incident with the sentry notwithstanding. He turned on the power to a SATCOM radio phone. A voice answered in English.

"Our sources at US CENTCOM are telling us of unusual activity over the Sinai Peninsula. The operation is already under way?" the American voice on the other end asked.

"You have heard of al Askari?" Idel asked. His jaw muscles twitched, and he tried to blink away the ache. He opened his mouth wide, hearing the mandible joint pop like distant gunshots.

"I've heard unsubstantiated rumors," the American answered.

"Well, he's on the other side of a two-inch-thick steel door. He's cut down several of my men, and he's working his way to kill us. He managed to get Unit 777 on his side, and they're trying to intercept our delivery vehicles," Idel stated.

There was a sigh. "I gave those Predators to you in the hopes that we could use them all. How many have we lost?"

"Too many," Idel said. "I'm bringing five back to perform a scorched earth campaign on this part of the plateau, but I've been exposed here."

Silence.

"Israel is not going to wade in blood," Idel told him, "but she will mourn the deaths of her children in the gas attacks that get through."

"We have nothing more to say. If you eliminate al Askari, you can contact me, face-to-face within a week."

The SATCOM locked out, signal dead.

Idel's jaw finally loosened. All of his tension leached from him at last.

He didn't know whether to feel free or to accept his coming doom.

BOLAN AND KALID WERE laying down heavy fire against the gunmen who had their backs to the sealed entrance of the command-and-control center. Bodies were strewed on the floor of the hall.

"Where did that girl go to?" Kalid asked impatiently.

"To get us an equalizer," Bolan answered.

Geren came around the corner, keeping tight to the dips and crags in the mine tunnel walls. Kalid ducked as rounds chipped the stone near his face, and he tried to see what Geren was holding.

She was busy stuffing a 40 mm round into the breech of a grenade launcher. It was the same grenade launcher that had nearly shredded the Executioner when he had made the mad dash that felt like an eternity before.

"Say hello to my little friend," Geren said to Kalid, racking the breech shut. "Fire in the hole!"

Bolan swept the tunnel with a covering burst and Geren took a step out, triggering the grenade launcher. A hollow thump thundered through the enclosed tunnel, sputtering out like the sound of bees buzzing as a thousand steel pellets went storming toward the entrance to the command-and-control center.

Geren yelped as a bullet clipped her, and Kalid reached out, grabbing her to him. He looked over his shoulder at the gory cloud of devastation wrought by her buckshot storm. He'd seen the round used in combat before, but never in such close quarters. The pellets didn't merely penetrate flesh once. They sliced through meat and bounced off stone and steel, like homicidal pinballs, rebounding and racking up deadly scores through human bodies.

What was left couldn't be described as human, and he glanced away.

"You were hit."

Geren looked down at her bicep, soaked with blood.

"That the only place you were hit?" Kalid asked.

She nodded.

"Alex, the grenades," Bolan said.

Kalid unslung his pouch of grenades and tossed them to the big soldier, who then moved to the door of the command-and-control center. The ex-blacksuit quickly began wadding up torn strips of cloth that used to belong to his ragged pants and plugged the gunshot wound. He wrapped them with another couple of straps, tying them down in place. "There."

"Get ready," Bolan warned.

Kalid watched Bolan press a radio-controlled detonator, and he covered Geren's head to protect her from the blast.

NATEG LOOKED AS THE PREDATORS suddenly jerked in response to an invisible stimulus.

"The nerve center's been breached!" Ekan shouted. "We've got a chance yet!"

"Israeli Air Defense to unidentified Egyptian helicopter, you are entering our sovereign airspace!" came the call that took the wind out of their momentary elation.

Ekan looked and saw that the Predators were still in action, moving and swinging lower to the ground. He glanced at Nateg.

"I've got two Israeli F-16s on radar, and they've got us lit up with their gunnery radar," Nateg said.

"This is Unit 777. We are in hot pursuit of unmanned drones entering your airspace," Ekan replied. "We don't have time to fool around!"

To punctuate his point, Ekan swung around the M-230 chain gun and took out another Predator drone that had been eluding him for some time. The machine exploded in midair.

"Cease fire and turn back to Egyptian airspace or be fired upon!" the F-16 pilot warned.

"Did you not see me shoot down something that's already in your airspace?" Ekan asked. "We're trying to prevent a war here!"

The F-16s came close, their engines roaring as they cut past the helicopter at a leisurely six hundred miles per hour. Nateg's vocabulary dissolved into a spewing of primitive curses and grunts as he tried to right the Apache.

"Remind me why we're trying to save them again," Nateg growled.

"Because we're all just trying to get along on this crazy little blue ball," Ekan answered.

The Apache shuddered and Nateg cried out. "Hydraulics are gone! We got clipped by a Predator!"

The cockpit shook, every screen suddenly visible in a wild double vision. Ekan tried to brace himself. "We've got more incoming!"

"I can't steer to get them off of us!"

"It was a long shot, Nateg."

"You aren't giving up already, are you?" Nateg asked.

The air shook again, two massive shapes cutting to the left and the right of the plummeting helicopter, 20 mm cannons splitting the air with lightning and thunder as they passed. None of the rounds came even close to the wounded Egyptian helicopter, and instants later, the cockpit stopped shaking enough for Ekan to see the drones vaporize from their radar.

"Unit 777 combat helicopter! Try to set down 350 meters ahead. The sand should be soft enough," the Israeli pilot called over the radio. "We'll take over from here and send search and rescue for you!"

"I see it!" Nateg growled, working the cyclic to keep the helicopter under control. "Ekan, what does damage control say? We're getting better!"

"The tail rotor took some damage. We lost one blade and another might have been bent, but is straightening out due to centrifugal force."

"Thank you Isaac Newton," Nateg whispered. "Fuel's gone!"

Ekan looked up. "Momentum."

"That's what I'm working on!" Nateg said. "Three fifty is going to be a long sail!"

The Apache soared toward the ground, the rotor blades still spinning. Ekan knew, though, every rotation bled speed, and cost their ability to stay aloft.

He braced for impact.

BOLAN WAS FIRST AT THE DOOR. It had been blown apart by SLAM munitions, which sliced through the two-inch steel as if it were butter. Gunfire ripped from the entrance, but the Executioner was laying down a sheet of fire from his AK-47, driving the shooters on the other end to cover or to an early grave. At least two of the command-and-control center defenders stumbled lifelessly to the ground under his fusillade.

Skidding to a halt, Bolan popped a grenade from his harness and lobbed it into the center, turning away, covering his ears and opening his mouth. The stun-shock bomb shook dust from the ceiling of the tunnel he was in, but the old rock continued to hold. He swung around as Kalid showed up on the other side of the doorway, M-4 probing the shadows.

"Surrender now!" Kalid called out. "We're just here for General Idel!"

Kalid lunged forward as sporadic gunshots flew through the hole Bolan had blasted.

"So much for surrender with honor," Bolan answered. He swung around and pounced through the hole in a baseball slide, AK-47 abandoned for the more portable and maneuverable .44 Magnum Desert Eagle.

An Egyptian renegade tried to track him as he dived behind a counter, but caught a single 240-grain hollowpoint above the bridge of his nose for his trouble. The defender tumbled to the cold hard floor.

Tucking tight and aiming, Bolan caught a second gunman trying to come around his blind side. Before the soldier could fully depress his trigger, the renegade Egyptian was perforated by a stream of M-4 fire from Kalid. The gunner tumbled lifelessly as the ex-blacksuit, an M-4 in each fist, sidestepped into the command center, both weapons ripping out long bursts.

"Down!" Bolan growled, popping up and sweeping for more targets.

Kalid cut loose with both of the M-4 rifles until they

locked empty. He let them drop and took a dive, bullets sizzling after him.

Kalid cried out, but Bolan didn't dare take his attention away from the enemy gunners. He dropped his Desert Eagle and pulled his Beretta as the big .44 Magnum ran empty.

"Alex?"

"Took one across the ribs!" Kalid called back.

"Take cover," Bolan ordered. He fed the hungry Beretta a fresh magazine now that no return fire was slamming into the communications console he was behind.

Bolan looked at the unit for a moment, then realized it had a U.S. Army Special Operations SATCOM phone on it. The shock of its appearance in the den of a madman distracted him.

"Striker!" Kalid bellowed.

Bolan whirled, bringing up his Beretta only to have it ripped from his hand, a rifle stock smashing his right hand with bone-breaking force.

He drew his injured hand back to his chest and looked into the face of a madman. Thick black hair and a mustache framed a round face that would have implied fatness on any other human being. From the neck down this man was built like a fireplug. He scrambled sideways, holding his rifle ready to chop down again. The Executioner kept his injured hand between himself and the enemy, preferring not to lose any more of his fighting parts when he could block with a wounded limb. It would hurt the healing process, but Bolan needed to survive to heal.

With a snarl, Kalid rose, launching himself at the goon, but the squat ape of a man pivoted, lashing out with a high kick catching Kalid in the jaw. The ex-blacksuit staggered, thrown to the floor in an unseemly tangle of uncontrolled limbs.

"Alex!" Bolan called out. He caught the rise and fall of his ally's chest. He was still breathing.

Gunfire barked from the doorway, and the mystery man

dived behind cover. Geren, holding a pistol in one hand, her other arm dangling, looked around.

"I'll watch Alex!" she called.

Bolan gave her a nod and scooped up his Beretta in his left hand.

Details from his quick observation of the enemy gave Bolan a clue as to the identity of the stocky soldier who had floored Kalid.

General's pips.

General Nahd Idel was too vain to take them off, even in the face of an assault. He could have slipped away.

"General Idel, your game is over. Make it easy on yourself!" Bolan called out.

There was a sharp laugh. "I know your legend, al Askari. You do not arrest men such as me, warriors of true vision."

"Then you know I usually end up taking down your delusional kind," Bolan answered.

"Delusional? I have risen through the ranks of the Egyptian army. I have built my own network of allies. I am seated at the right hand of a genius who will take your nation and make it a seat of power that we will be able to coexist with," Idel answered.

Bolan stopped, spotting the rows of computers linked together on mess tables. He scanned them quickly and found power bars on the end of each. He began firing, sparks spraying as electricity shorted out.

"What are you doing?" Idel yelled.

"Your Predators have been defanged!" Bolan announced.

MAJOR FESJAD LOOKED UP as the five drones sailed through the skies. Instead of swinging down toward the cliff face, they continued flying straight and true, unwavering in their course.

"They broke through!" Fesjad announced. "Get in there now! I don't care if Colonel Stone told us to hold back."

"On it!" Nomad called out. "We spotted a tunnel in from one of the nests on night vision."

"Go," Fesjad ordered.

He switched frequencies. "Nova to Deathbird. Nova to Deathbird. Are you still operating?"

Static.

Fesjad tried another frequency. "Nova to Deathbird. Come in."

Empty silence.

Fesjad swallowed hard. "Ekan!"

"We're here."

Fesjad grinned. "And the Predators heading for Israeli airspace?"

"Tell 'em, boys…" Ekan answered.

"This is IADF, Major Rose. Once the craft stopped evasive maneuvers, it was a turkey shoot," came the reply.

"Had to be diplomatic-like and tell our neighbors about the pest problem," Ekan cut in.

"Naturally," Fesjad answered. "We'll talk about the breach in protocol back at the base."

"I think the Americans have a term that fits this," Rose called over the radio.

"What's that?" Fesjad asked.

"Peace out, y'awl," Rose answered.

Fesjad grinned from ear to ear. "Peace out, Major Rose."

THE AIR IN THE CAVE trembled for a moment, mostly from the echoes of the pistol shattering the surge protectors, but the Executioner could still imagine part of that tremor as the underlying rage set to explode from General Idel. He braced himself, Beretta at the ready as he moved slowly, tracking around the maze of the command center, muzzle following his icy eyes in the semidarkness.

Movement flashed in the corner of his eye, and even before the gunshot roared, Bolan hit the floor, Beretta swinging up and seeking human flesh. Both bullets missed their mark, a curse in Arabic letting him know how close his own fire was. He scrambled on all fours, crawling under the computer tables, shoving aside chairs to get toward Idel in a straight line without exposing himself.

Idel had other plans. Dropping down and spotting Bolan, he plowed along, burrowing his way past chairs and cables. Computers jerked and fell as he charged, then Bolan saw the flash of the rogue Egyptian's pistol again. There was no time to avoid the gunshots, even though he threw himself to one side, triggering his own Beretta.

Slugs bounced off the floor at oblique angles, dashing off behind the Executioner, tracking along the stony ground. Two bullets sliced Bolan's right arm, and he went crashing onto his face, Beretta tumbling from his left hand. He clutched the bloodied arm, cursing the loss of his pistol.

Idel gave a growl of satisfaction, his booted feet stomping toward the end of the row of tables.

Bolan twisted, letting go of his injured arm and grabbing a rolling chair. He gave it a quick spin and side-kicked it hard. Idel sprinted around the corner, and the chair rammed into him, tripping him up. The fireplug frame of the Egyptian general went tumbling to the ground, the jarring impact popping his pistol free.

Idel was faster and healthier, though. Bolan looked at him and realized that the general had all the advantages. The stocky renegade was on his feet just a few seconds faster than Bolan.

Idel hadn't suffered multiple concussions in the past week.

Idel's hand wasn't shattered.

Idel didn't give any indication that he felt like lying down and closing his eyes forever.

"This is al Askari? A bloody rag of a man? How could you

think you could stop me?" Idel asked. He lashed out with a stabbing left. Bolan ducked it and got caught by a right cross, a stunning blow that rocked him. He stumbled hard against a computer station, the monitor spilling to the floor with a resounding crash.

Idel was moving in quickly, not giving Bolan a chance to rest and recover. The soldier's left hand groped for something and he came up with the cord of the computer's mouse, swinging it hard. The lightweight plastic bounced off of Idel's head. Shock more than pain made him step backward, and Bolan let the cord go. He bent his left arm to protect his chest, fist at the chin, ready to fight to the last, feet splayed.

Idel lunged again, a sharp kick smashing Bolan in the bicep. The Executioner grunted, dropping to one knee.

"You're just a weak, bleeding man, so fallible that you murdered those who would be your allies," Idel snarled.

"That is no mere man!" a weak voice croaked.

Idel looked to the source of the echoing voice of Alex Kalid, confused.

Bolan snarled. "Unit 777 not only forgave me my mistake, they are risking their lives outside to make sure you don't escape."

Idel lowered his head, eyes narrowed. "They're fools."

Bolan lashed out with a kick, but the desperate attack missed. Sweat beaded on the forehead of the Egyptian madman as he shuffled his feet, keeping out of range of Bolan's legs.

The Egyptian lashed out with his own kick, but Bolan had retreated.

The soldier feinted with his left foot, then dropped to it, spin-kicking hard with his right foot. His boot sole caught Idel in the chest, driving him backward.

Idel lunged at him, fists flashing, but Bolan's left forearm swatted them aside, deflecting their force. Sweat was drenching the Executioner through and through. He snapped his right knee up at Idel who barely had the quickness to block the blow. Bolan instead settled for a left toe to the shin. He continued, unabated. He snapped out two quick left kicks, and when Idel finished reacting to them, he brought his left fist crashing in a backhand across Idel's jaw.

Idel charged, his shoulder ramming the Executioner in the chest. But Bolan slammed his elbow hard between the Egyptian's shoulder blades, feeling bone dislocate. Idel screamed in piercing agony. Bolan grabbed him by his belt and pivoted, hurling him against the stone wall of the command center, his head bouncing off the wall.

Bolan stepped toward the stunned Egyptian.

"You fool…" Idel sputtered. "You think you've won, but I'm only the first wave."

Bolan brought down his boot on Idel's throat with merciless force, crushing windpipe and smashing vertebrae in one savage stomp. The master of the devil's tools was served the justice of the Executioner.

Exactly three seconds later, exhaustion and blood loss had him staggering against the wall. "Alex?"

"I'm here," Kalid said.

The ex-blacksuit and Geren limped to his side.

The Executioner regarded them for a long, painful moment. "Let's get out of this rat's nest."

The Executioner, leaning on his friends, worked his way out of the darkness, all the while thinking about Idel's promise of further madmen to follow.

Bolan remembered the SATCOM radio. It was United States military issue, and it would be useless for backtracking Idel's sponsors. The renegade general had put a 9 mm bullet through every single component that could hold a memory of transmissions.

A new age of evil wanted to reform the world, and the plot

to throw Egypt and Israel into bloody war was only one step in this overarching plan.

But, if the true architects of terror wanted to continue their battle with him, Mack Bolan would not back down. They'd have to kill him first.

Even if they did bring down the Executioner, he had his arms around a small sampling of the kind of allies who would continue to make sacrifices and fight to save the day. Men like Anwar Fesjad, Atef Fesjad, the pilots Nateg and Ekan and the rest of Unit 777.

And most importantly, the two human beings who were giving the wounded soldier support after this bloody conflict.

No.

Mack Bolan would only back down when his body slipped into its grave. Until then, he intended to keep living and fighting as large as he could.

James Axler
Outlanders®

CHILDREN OF
THE SERPENT

After 4,000 years the kings return to claim their kingdom: Earth.

**He is a being of inhuman evil, a melding of dragon, myth and machine.
He is Lord Enlil, ruler of the Overlords. As the barons evolve into
creatures infinitely more dangerous than the egomaniacs who ruled
from the safety of their towers, Tiamat, safeguarding the ancient race,
is now the key to the fruition of their plan. Kane and the Cerberus
exiles, pledged to free humanity from millennia of manipulation, face
a desperate—perhaps impossible—task: stop Enlil and the Overlords
from reaching the mother ship...and claiming Earth as theirs.**

Available May 2005 at your favorite retailer.

GOLD
EAGLE®

GOUT33

Black Harvest

**Available March 2005
at your favorite retail outlet**

Emerging from a gateway in the Midwest, Ryan Cawdor senses trouble within the well-fortified ville of a local baron, whose understanding of preDark medicine may be their one chance to save a wounded Jak. But while his whitecoats can make the drugs that heal, the baron knows the real power and money is in the hardcore Deathlands jolt. And where drugs and riches go, death shadows every step, no matter which side of a firefight you stand on....

In the Deathlands, tomorrow is never just another day.

GOLD EAGLE

GDL69

TAKE 'EM FREE

2 action-packed novels plus a mystery bonus

NO RISK

NO OBLIGATION TO BUY